MARION CATTERALL

DIAMOND MEDIA PRESS CO.
1-747-998-2352
https://www.diamondmediapressco.com/

ISBN Paperback: 978-1-951302-40-5

To my dearest husband William, my 2 sons
David and Stephen and to my 3 beautiful
girls Jennifer, Claire and Sarah with
all my love and affection.

CONTENTS

CHAPTER 1

Introduction

I am Christine Delaney, and this is my story.

I was a forty-four-year old woman who had lost her husband two years prior. We had had a loving relationship and a good marriage. We did everything together and had a good social network with many friends, all of them couples, and relatives, all of them couples. Holidays, outings, escorted coach holidays, going for meals, and seeing shows – the list was endless.

There was no sexual intimacy in our relationship, in large part because of my husband's medication and his many health issues. This was not an issue, as I had never really been interested in that side of married life. I would not say that I was frigid but rather that I could not see what all the fuss was about in sex.

When my husband died, like many thousands of women, I found that I had no close single friends to turn to, to help me start a new way of living. All the couples we knew were sympathetic to my situation and were always inviting me to join them for various outings, but it did not rest correct for me and I gently turned down the majority of offers.

One beautiful couple with whom I felt completely relaxed was my sister Ruth and her husband, Matt. I would go anywhere with them, and indeed, I did. Ruth was my sister, and she was also my best friend. Our families were close, so I could turn to Ruth for anything.

I am of medium height and build. I have short blond hair and blue eyes.

I considered myself to be reasonably attractive for my age. I had breasts, not boobs. I had never had cleavage. I dressed accordingly, making the best of my attributes.

I was educated by the nuns of a convent called The Convent of the Holy Child Jesus. They sucked eleven-year- old girls in and spit them out at the age of seventeen or eighteen as well-educated young ladies.

I spent most of my working life running our family haulage company. As my husband worked less, I worked more. I achieved accountancy status with the help of our accountant working with NVQ modules. With my banking background, I considered myself to be a businesswoman, and I was proud of that.

Our haulage business failed during the recession. I was relieved because the pressure of keeping it going and having an invalid husband was too much for me to cope with. The day I called in the receivers was the first day in many could relax. My husband and I took this opportunity to retire fully. We travelled far and wide and saw and experienced everything we could.

I had two wonderful children, a son and a daughter. I did not see much of my son, but my daughter, Beth, and her partner lived very close to me. Their two children, my beautiful grandchildren, were a joy to me.

I had always had good health, but one health issue would not go away. In a period of thirteen months, I had had both my hips replaced. The second hip replacement – the right– had not gone according to plan. The bones in this right leg were badly damaged with osteoarthritis. I was left with a good repair to this leg, but I had to be careful and use a crutch at all times to give me the support that my leg could not. This did not bother me at all. I was just so grateful that I was mobile.

I had restructured my life now. I kept myself busy with helping my daughter and her friends. She had many, many friends; to some of them, I was like a second mum. They were all so busy, all of them working with children and not having time to stop juggling what life threw them to survive.

I was there for school duties – picking up and dropping off. I was a troubleshooter when things went wrong. During the rest of my time, I took long walks with my beloved little pug dog, shopped, watched television, painted my nails, went to the hairdresser, gardened, and more.

I lived in a lovely, three-bedroom, detached dormer bungalow on an estate in a beautiful rural area of England. I had lived in this bungalow for over forty years, and I had never tired of it. To the front of the bungalow was the road and my driveway. To the rear were fields, woods, pine tree areas, and walks that led to the cove inlets on the coast where the tide washed them from time to time.

My bungalow provided me with all the security I needed as a Woman on her own. I was proud of it, felt secure in it, and had many happy memories in it, and I was comfortable there.

4

CHAPTER 2

First Meeting

It was two weeks from Beth and her partner, Martin's, wedding day. It was all systems go. This coming weekend was the home hen do. That is a do for all the oldies who had not gone on the abroad hen do. There were many going, including most of the abroad hen do – me; Ruth; Martin's mum, aunty, and grandma; and many other older friends and relatives. A coach had been booked to pick us up at a centralised place and take us all to the venue where there was dinner, dancing, a comedian, a live band, and a DJ.

I was so excited and so looking forward to it. It had been quite a while since I had been to anything like this. I had purposely bought a short-sleeved shirtwaist dress that was black-and-light-blue checked. I paired it with black tights and shoes, a crystal choker necklace and matching earrings, a fancy watch, and a bracelet. I had a soft blue woollen wrap in lieu of a coat. I was all ready for this women-only night.

Finally, the day arrived. I went to the hairdresser, did my nails, and had a bath and an afternoon nap to help me keep my evening strength up. As arranged, Martin picked me up and took me to the meeting point for the coach. All the girls were there.

We all boarded the coach. Everyone was in good spirits and looking forward to a good evening. The younger women were already giddy and loud. When I was their age, it was not proper to behave like that. I laughed at them. They showed that they were enjoying life, so good on them.

We arrived at the venue, a large hotel that had entertainment suites as well as wedding reception suites, conference centres, and more. We left the coach and entered the large building. Straight ahead was the meeting area and foyer. The bar was situated on this level and was surrounded by all women. It seemed as though the promoters put on these women-only hen dos from time to time. I glanced over the balcony to see the stage, the dance floor, and the long rows of tables, each marked with the hen's surname. I located the tables reserved for our party. With my mobility, I had to be seated on the end of a row. I could not be centralised and having to repeatedly get up and down. I told Ruth to buy us drinks, and though not allowed, I went down a level to the tables and placed my wrap on a chair at the end of the row. On the opposite chair, I placed Ruth's coat. I returned to the bar and enjoyed my glass of wine. At the end of each row, a small bucket with sand in it had been placed. In this were flags on sticks, the idea being that once everyone had been seated, if anyone required anything further, you placed the flag in the bucket. I thought this was a brilliant idea and one that worked perfectly well all evening.

After quite a wait, we were all called to our tables. Ruth immediately put the flag into the bucket, and when our waiter came, she ordered a bottle of wine. She insisted that it worked out cheaper than buying by the glass. I knew that Ruth would enjoy the majority of the bottle of wine. One or two glasses of wine was more than enough for me.

The food was excellent, served quickly and with precision. After the meal, the comedian came on to entertain us while the band prepared the stage with all its instruments. The comedian was very good, dirty, and loud, and the girls loved it. Now, it was time for the band. Most of the girls were already on the dance f loor, dancing to the DJ's music. My party of girls was pulling at me to get me up to dance with them. Most of them were drunk but really enjoying themselves. Ruth was already on the dance f loor, dancing away and waiting for the band to come on. I knew that the most sensible thing that I could do was to get away from the table and move somewhere quieter.

I moved to the back of the dance f loor room and to the side of the stage. It was quieter there. Nobody could see me, and I could sit and enjoy the band without the girls making nuisances of themselves. When the band started playing, I was thrilled by the sound and the volume of their instruments. They were very, very good. I put my crutch to one side and stood to watch them.

It was then that I noticed a guy walking back and forth at the back of the stage. He was checking his tablet and the computers on stage, all the leads, and all the lighting lamps. He was tall, looked to be in his fifties, and had a good build with dark hair and silver highlights. He was well-dressed and good looking, and he even had a diamond – a large one – studded in one of his ears. I watched him for some time while listening to the band.

He turned and started to walk across the back of the stage toward where I was stood. Our eyes met, and electricity went right through me. He smiled and winked, and I smiled and nodded. He stood at the end of the stage only yards from where I was stood, and he started a dance move – two small steps to the right and two small steps to the left while holding his hands at shoulder height and moving gently to the rhythm. His eyes never left mine, and the electricity I felt was so strong. He beckoned me to copy his little dance routine. I laughed and pointed to my crutch. He continued to beckon me to join him with his dance moves and surprised me by picking up a trumpet and playing a solo part for the band.

My goodness, could he play that trumpet! So loud, so clear, so beautiful. He could make that trumpet sing. It was obvious that he was an accomplished musician and an extremely good trumpet player. When he had finished his solo, he restarted his dance routine, again beckoning me to join in. This time, I did join in. Two small steps to the right and two small steps to the left with my hands at shoulder height. I moved in time to his movements and the beat of the music. He picked up his trumpet and started playing his next piece of music. It all happened so quickly. The band finished, the curtain came round the stage, all the lights came on, and the DJ thanked the band. Disco music took over.

I returned to my seat. Everyone was preparing to leave. Beth and a few of the girls came rushing back, saying that we had about three-quarters of an hour before the coach was due to arrive and that they were to go to the bar in the foyer for a few more drinks. Ruth said that she had phoned her husband and he was on his way to pick her up. She hurried away. I went to the loo to freshen up, put lipstick on, straighten my hair, and catch my breath.

That trumpet player had messed with my mind. I could not stop thinking about him and the strong connection I thought we had made. There was definitely some attraction between us.

I came out of the loo into the foyer, and I could see through the glass doors where the coaches were to park. There were so many girls and women outside, and the coaches had started to arrive. It looked as if there was going to be gridlock with all the coaches arriving at the same time. I saw the trumpet player walking towards me, and I think my heart stopped. He grabbed me round my waist, put my arm on his shoulder, and held my other hand close to his chest like you do when doing a slow waltz. He had also placed my crutch in a safe place on the f loor.

We started to dance to the DJ's music. We both laughed as we realised that we were really quite good dancing together, both of us appreciating the beats of the records. In a very strong French accent, he said, "I am Henri Chartress."

I replied, "I am Christine Delaney."

"Have you a husband?" he said.

"No, I have not," I replied.

"Have you got a partner?" he asked.

"No, I have not," I replied with a smile, wondering whether he had a partner.

"Then I shall take you home. You cannot go home on a coach. You can see for yourself how bad it is out there. It is worse than a war zone."

"Sorry, Henri. I have a daughter who is a hen, and I must make sure that she and her party get home safely."

I knew he was going to kiss me, so I raised my face towards him as he placed his lips on mine. Softly and gently, he kissed me seductively. The thrill of that kiss went through all of my body, even to my fingers and toes. I then left to find Beth and the girls.

It was a disgrace outside; too many coaches for the parking area. Everyone was trying to locate her coach. Some women were getting sick in the plants, some were arguing, and some crying due to drinking too much.

I could not find Beth or even see any girls from our party. I began to panic. I was being knocked around by the sheer volume of people. I tried to take my mobile out of my small crossover bag, but I could not get to it. I started to feel frightened, hoping that I did not lose my footing, and I held on tight to my crutch. Thankfully, I saw Beth. She was near a wall. At the same time, I felt Henri holding me round my waist. "You are coming with me whether you want to or not," he said with his beautiful French accent. He fought his way through the sea of women with me holding on to him until we reached a quieter area near the staff car park. He let me go. "My car is over there near to the main road. Come with me, and I will take you home." He said this with a beautiful smile across his face, and I smiled in return.

"Wait," I said. "Please help me get my mobile out as I need to speak to my daughter, Beth." We both struggled to retrieve the phone, and we both laughed at our ridiculous efforts to get the damn phone. At last, Henri had it in his hand, and he passed it to me. I immediately phoned her, and she answered. I checked with her that she was OK and told her that I had a lift home. She answered that together with her friends, she was to continue the party back at her house. Ugh!

Henri pointed to his car, and we walked towards it. It was a large Mercedes, a beauty. He opened the passenger door, put my crutch into the back seat, and started to help me in when I shouted in protest. "What is the matter?" he said with concern.

I laughed and said, "Bucket seats! If you manage to get me in it, I am not sure you will be able to get me out of it."

He laughed and said, "I agree with what you are saying. I sometimes struggle. Come. I will put you in, and I will get you out." By this time, we were both a bit giddy. He held me close as he slid me down into the seat. Feeling him holding me so close sent shivers down my body. It was a lovely sensation. He closed the passenger door, got into the driver's side and closed his door, and started the engine. Before he moved, he turned to look at me for directions. Those eyes. Our eyes met and locked. For a moment, I thought I saw Henri gasp. Perhaps he felt what I felt – electricity zapping through my whole body.

"Turn left, and head down the main road. I will tell you when to turn off," I said. I was admiring the inside of this motor, so classy all leather. There was jazz playing on the radio. "Turn right, and follow the road to the top. There, you can pull into my drive," I said.

He turned his engine off, came round to the passenger side, opened the door, placed both his arms round my waist, and said, "Help me pull you up." We both started laughing again, getting giddy with the situation. He tried twice, and on the third time, he succeeded in lifting me out and put me down by the car. He pushed me up against the side of the car, pressed hard against me, and kissed me, not a gentle slow one but a hard demanding sensual kiss to which I responded. I kissed him back, with the same urgency I could feel from Henri.

I opened my front door, turned on all the lights, and went into my kitchen and breakfast room. Henri followed and went from room to room, having a really good look around. "Oh, mon dieu," he said with some other French exclamations. I had no idea what they meant. At that point, I remembered that I still had my bed in the lounge. It had been moved into the lounge after I had had my recent surgery. I could not manage the stairs, and the toilet was on the lounge level, so it made sense to move my bed into the lounge. Since I was comfortable with that arrangement, I was not ready to take the bed upstairs.

I rushed into the lounge to explain why the room was as it was. He was grinning, and I responded with a scolding look. We both laughed again.

It was at that moment that I realised that Henri might want to have sex with me. I could under no circumstances do that. He made a lunge at me, and I quickly made an exit. I knew I had to tell him that it was coffee or nothing!

"Henri, I need to talk to you. Please listen. I have not been with a man for many, many years. I do not know how to respond to you or what to do. I feel very uncomfortable and a little frightened by this situation. I find you extremely attractive and very sexy, but I do not want sex, so it is coffee or nothing," I said.

"That is all right," he said as he sat on one of the large leather chairs in my lounge. "I do not want coffee," he said, and we both laughed. I was embarrassed and wished he would go. "Just listen to me now," he said, his eyes firmly on mine. Oh, those eyes. "What if I take it very gently and slowly? At intervals, I will ask if you are OK, and if you say yes, I will continue, but if you say no, I will stop straight away. I will not force you to do anything that you do not want to do, and I will not hurt you. What do you think?"

I thought about life being full of missed opportunities. "Yes, I will try to enjoy what you can offer."

"Bon, bon," he exclaimed loudly.

He sat on the edge of the bed with his legs open to where he pulled me in between them and started to undo my dress buttons. His eyes never left mine. My dress fell to the f loor where I kicked it away. I had a silk slip underneath my clothing as I very rarely wore a bra. His hands slid up and down my silk slip, stopping to hold my breasts and play with my nipples. I gasped and held my breath. His hands now running up my legs and pulling down my tights and knickers, and I got free of them and kicked them away.

"Are you OK?" he said, waiting for my answer.

"Yes, I replied." He pulled me down to his face by pulling on my breasts, hard but not hurting me, and kissed me hard and long. I stood up as he stood up, and he told me to lie on the bed as he took his clothes off. He knelt beside me and moved my delicate leg out of harm's way. He then moved my other leg out sideways as well. I could see his penis, hard and throbbing.

He asked again if I was OK, this time with a smile, and I replied, also with a smile, that I was.

He lay at my side, taking his weight on his shoulders and hips, and with one arm under my head, he pulled on my hair. The other hand was between my legs playing with my clitoris. He nibbled my nipples and then kissed me so seductively, his tongue in and outside my mouth. I knew that I was very near coming – that is, reaching a climax. "I am not going to ask if you are OK," he said. "It is too late now," and with that, he slid his penis inside me. With perfect precision, he moved inside me making me feel so much pleasure that I thought I could take no more. I could not catch my breath, and I exploded, climaxing dramatically. I had never climaxed like that ever. Henri continued to move with more urgency, and he came, giving a very heavy sigh. He then moved onto the pillow at the side of me. I had just had a huge, explosive orgasm.

We lay still for a little while. I was wet all over. I turned to him as he turned to me, and we simultaneously said, "Wow!" We laughed uncontrollably.

"I have never felt anything like that before. So intense! Wow!" said Henri.

"Christine, I now have to ask," he said, laughing. "How was it for you?"

"OK. Yes, it was OK," I replied with laugher.

"Henri, I now have to ask how it was for you," I said.

"Yes, it was OK," he replied, still laughing.

He got up off the bed, threw some covers on me, and went into the bathroom. I lay there feeling quite pleased with all of this. When he returned, he was nearly fully dressed, and as he put his shoes on, he asked me for my mobile. I could not see it anywhere amongst all the clothes, shoes, and bedding on the f loor. I knew my mobile number, but it was my mobile he had asked for, and I thought it best to be left like that. He fastened his pants and belt and straightened his shirt and bent over and kissed me quickly and gently on my lips. The front door closed with a bang. He was gone!

I should have felt disgusted with myself. I should have

felt ashamed. I should have felt dirty and cheap, but I did not. Instead, I felt proud.

I could have shouted it to everyone that I was so proud of myself for having achieved a massive orgasm, for the first time and at my age. I then drifted into a calm sleep.

I woke to the sun coming into the room, the sound of the birds singing, and the strong smell of sex. I got up, put my bathrobe on, stripped the sheets, placed the bedding into the washing machine, let the dog out, had a shower, and dried my hair. I then put clean linen onto the bed and got dressed. With my makeup on and my hair done, I enjoyed toast and coffee.

I felt as if a light had been switched on inside. Everything seemed brighter and sounded better, and I felt that I had courage to try anything now.

Thank you, thank you, Monsieur Henri Chartress.

The phone rang. It was Beth, asking had I gotten home OK. I said that I had, and she asked whether I had invited him in for coffee. I said yes and was met with silence. I knew she had more questions, but not to her mother, so she changed the subject, telling me that most of her friends were quite ill this morning, including herself. I told her I felt brilliant, and it was a wonderful night that went extremely well. Relieved, she hung up.

It was then that I realised I could not continue living as I had been. I had made a life for myself after my husband died. I now knew that the life I had made for myself was completely inadequate. Some changes had to be made, some dramatic changes.

I set off, taking the dog for a walk. I had a lot of thinking to do. One thing that I did know was that I had to get away from my bungalow. One obvious place to go was northern Spain.

Some years before my husband died, we purchased a large mobile home. It was beautiful and large, with three bedrooms, a lounge and dining area, a fully equipped kitchen, shower room, and two toilets with views to die for. It was surrounded by a large wooden decking with a shed that housed a washing machine.

It was situated on a rural site in northern Spain, not far from the French border, about thirty minutes from the coast and all the coastal resorts. It was a beautiful area in the Pyrenees on the outskirts of a quaint, small, pretty Spanish village. The mobile home was on a high point on the site, hence the magnificent views it had.

The site housed many mobile homes and caravans, but each plot was large and privately situated. I knew many people on this site of all nationalities, but one person I knew very well on this site was Ruth. Ruth and her husband had been there for years, travelling back and forward to England but staying the majority of their time in Spain.

My husband had always driven to Spain, taking various routes, but since we got the dog, we always took Le Shuttle. It was easier as we never had to leave the car, and Doggy had us with him all of the journey. What I had to do now was to get enough courage to drive all through France and into Spain with an overnight hotel in France. Making this journey on my own was quite a feat and possibly a little risky.

I ruled out the mobile home when my husband died, so I closed it up and just left it there for other family members to use. I was not confident enough to drive all the way through

France on my own to get there. Well, that attitude had just changed!

When we returned from our walk, I put the dog in his pen and phoned Ruth to see when she was next travelling to Spain. She informed me that she was f lying out straight after the wedding. When I told Ruth that I would be joining them in Spain for a month or two, she was delighted but concerned about me travelling alone. She told me to f ly out with them, but I explained that I needed to bring doggy with me for companionship and security and that I was not going to put him in kennels. Ruth and her husband had a car permanently in Spain, so they could f ly back and forth from home.

Within one hour of speaking with Ruth, I had booked the Le Shuttle, the French hotel, my hair appointment, the vet for the dog's passport update, and a service for my car. I was so pleased with myself and so excited.

Now I could concentrate on Beth's wedding.

The wedding was brilliant. Nothing went wrong. Even the weather was kind to us. After the reception, I came home, climbed into bed, and slept. It was finally all over. Two years in the planning, and it was over within one day.

The six days leading up to my journey allowed me to take care of all my appointments. I went on a shopping spree, which I had never done before, and bought a complete outfit of new clothes. I replaced all of my holiday wear. Everything, including shorts, evening dresses, sun hats, shoes, sandals, knickers, and tops, was new. I put everything into the boot of the car. I bought new makeup, new face creams, new perfume, and new leather and crystal jewellery. Also in the boot of the car, I put an overnight bag and a bag for doggy. The cool bag had to be completed on the morning of our departure.

The day had finally arrived, the day I was to start my journey from home to my mobile home in Spain.

I woke to sunshine and birds singing. After showering, I dressed in slacks, a shirt, and a soft, baggy jumper. I finalised the cool box and put it into boot of car. Doggy was buckled in in the back seat. All paperwork had been checked and double-checked. Passports, money, and all the rest were in order. The bungalow windows and doors had all been locked, and all water and electricity had been turned off.

I sat in the car, checked that doggy was OK, and left. I had booked a lunchtime train on Le Shuttle, giving me six to seven hours to get to the French motel at Vierzon, a town on the others side of Paris. With two hours to get to Le Shuttle, I settled down to drive there, taking my time. My best ever friend was beside me, TomTom. She had never let me or my husband down. The first stop was to be a comfort stop at the services just before the Le Shuttle terminal.

Before I knew it, I was pulling into the services. After the comfort break, we resumed our journey. I drove straight up the slip road, had a manual booking in, chose which train we wanted, followed the car lane as instructed, and drove onto the car carrier. Off we went. So easy, but we still had a long way to go.

We drove off the train and onto the French roads. I had previously programmed TomTom, and I carried out all her instructions without question. I just had to keep reminding myself that I had to be on the opposite side of the road. The road towards Paris was very quiet, and I settled down to do a few hundred miles before she spoke to me again.

I could tell we were nearing Paris as the traffic was increasing in volume. I pulled into a large services for a comfort stop.

The nearer we got to Paris and the Peripherique, the Paris Ring Road, Tom Tom's instructions increased. By the time we were on the Peripherique, Tom Tom's instructions were fast and furious. I had no time to think. I just kept up with the speed of the traffic, going under the city in tunnels similar to the one Diana had been killed in. Tom Tom instructed me to take the Port de la Italia exit, and I knew then that I had nearly completed crossing through Paris. I kept driving, keeping up with other motorists, and the road widened. We were then on a motorway heading towards Vierzon. I had done it! One hour later, Tom Tom told me I had reached my destination. There in front of me was the motel I had booked for the night.

I booked in at the reception and was given a key code. I took what I needed for the night into the motel and relaxed.

It was a beautiful evening. At about seven, the sun was still shining so I took doggy for quite a long walk to tire him out. On return to the room, I fed and watered doggy and fed and watered me. A pot noodle, sandwich, and a cup of tea – what more could I have wanted?

The next morning, I showered and dressed, walked and fed doggy, and locked him in the car while I had breakfast at an outside table where I could see him. Tom Tom said I was about eight hours from my mobile home, taking the route straight down the centre of France and over the border into Spain. This route was the quietest.

We resumed our journey, and according to my reckoning, we were due to arrive at my mobile home by mid- to late afternoon. Ruth texting me for progress reports.

This part of the journey was beautiful, with rolling fields, chateaus, valleys, hills, and small towns. It had it all. I stopped for a couple of comfort stops and gave doggy some longer walks.

We arrived at the Spanish border, and half an hour later, I parked at my mobile home. I had arrived.

I had not even had time to take doggy out of the car when Ruth and Matt were running up the hill to greet me. They were so pleased to see me there, safe and sound.

They collected all my bags out of the car. Doggy and I climbed up the steps onto my decking and closed the decking gate behind us. I walked into my mobile home. It looked so beautiful in the sunshine. Ruth had opened it up and set up all the decking furniture. There were four large sun loungers, a dining table and chairs under the canopy, a coffee table with two small chairs, and a f lat sun lounger. I immediately found the tablecloth for the outside dining table and put it in place with a small artificial vase of f lowers in the centre. The decking looked superb. I wandered through the rooms. They all looked immaculate and smart. I was proud of it all, so I knew I would be happy staying here for as long as I would want to. I had completed the journey, so I could do it again, with no problem at all.

I had a great reception from all the other residents. Over the next few weeks, I found myself being invited to meals out, long walks, group get-togethers with plenty of wine, barbeques, and many more outings.

On this rural site, there were all nationalities, single people, married people, and same-sex couples, all with their own stories to tell. I quickly made friends with most of them. In particular, I spent time with a single man called Stanley, Ruth and Matt, a couple called Dee and Marcus, and a single women called Cleo.

Over the following year, I travelled back and forward to Spain several times, staying for a few months a time. I loved every minute of it all.

CHAPTER 3

Second and Subsequent Meetings

On my first visit of the next year, a group of residents made arrangements for us all to go to the music festival in the nearby coastal resort. There was to be a meal first, and we would then head up to the village of Sant Marti to enjoy some music and dancing. I was so looking forward to this.

On the day of this outing, I dressed in my most beautiful dress. With my glorious tan, I thought I looked fantastic.

We had a party of twelve, including Ruth and myself. We made our way in a convoy of cars to the coast and had a delicious meal with plenty of local wine. From there, we drove to the village of Sant Marti, a pretty village that overlooked the beaches and sea. We arranged seating for us all at the edge of an area being used as a dance f loor. The stage area for the musicians was a little way from where we were, but it was fine. More drinks followed.

It was then that I heard the trumpet solo Henri played at Beth's hen night. By body ran cold. Could it be that he was here performing? I jumped out of my seat and fought my way to the stage area. I just had to see if it was Henri. Disappointment set in when I saw that it was someone else. I felt so def lated and made my way back to my party of people. I was just about to sit on my chair when I saw him.

There he was, standing and talking to people. At the same time as I saw him, he saw me. With no hesitation from either of us, we made our way to meet, which we did on the dance f loor.

I felt his arms round me, and his eyes fixed on mine. Oh, those eyes. We kissed as if we were lost and now found. My whole body felt tingles and electricity. We must have kissed for some time, and we started to dance to the music. "I have thought of you so often since that night," said Henri. "I was going to come back to where you lived, but life and time got in the way. What are you doing here?" he asked.

"I have a mobile home in this area that I visit over the warmer months," I replied.

"I live just over the border in France, less than an hour away, and I did not know you were here. Now I know I can visit you whenever. That is brilliant. I do not want to lose touch with you again," he said.

As we held each other close and danced to the music, I was so excited. I could tell that Henri was really aroused. "Have you got a husband?" he asked.

"No, I have not," I replied.

"Have you got a partner?" he asked.

"No, I have not," I answered.

All this was as before, and I waited and smiled as he asked, "Can I take you home?"

"Yes, please," I answered, smiling at those large, dark eyes that threw electricity at me. He then asked me to make my apologies to my party and meet him at the yellow door in the corner of the room. He said he would do the same. We separated to make our excuses.

I had just reached the yellow door when I heard Henri right behind me. The yellow door opened to the outside area with a car park at the bottom of a small hill. "Can you manage this hill? My car is just on the left."

"Yes," I replied, and we hugged each other and my crutch all the way down.

"That is my car there," he said, pointing to a large Mercedes.

I laughed as I said, "I thought as much."

He opened the passenger side and put my crutch on the back seat. I laughed again as I made the same comment about bucket seats. Henri also laughed, lifted me up, and slid me in the seat. "Well done," I said.

He opened the driver's door, got in, turned the engine on, turned to me, looked me straight in my eyes, and asked me for directions to my mobile home. I was not exactly sure how to get there, so I told him if he could get onto the main French\ Spanish highway, I would recognise the mountain turnoff. This he did and at quite a speed. I did recognise the turnoff, which Henri took, and we passed the village into the rural site, passed the swimming pool, went round the bend and up the small hill, and stopped at the base of my decking steps.

We closing decking gate for doggy, put the key in the door, and went inside. Henri, like before, wandered from room to room, muttering words in French. "It is beautiful, and the views must be spectacular," he said as he made a grab for me. Feeling his arms round me with his body pushed hard up against me and his breath on my face and his lips on mine was erotic.

It was not long before I was on my bed minus my clothes. Henri took his clothes off and adjusted my position so as to protect my poorly leg. My other leg was taken out sideways. From there, Henri slowly manoeuvred himself up my body. With kisses, bites, licks, and strokes, he covered every inch of my naked body. By the time he actually started to fuck me, I was so sensitive and excited that it was not long before I exploded into my climax. Henri continued to move until he also came. He moved over next to me, and both of us said, "Wow," simultaneously, just as we had done once before. This time, though, we did not laugh but held each other very close. Henri went to the shower room, and when he returned, he was fully dressed. He told me that he would call on me now that he knew where I was staying and gave me a quick kiss. The outside door closed, and he was gone. Just as before, only I knew I would be seeing him again this time.

About a week later, after getting up very early, putting doggy on decking, and taking a shower, I walked through to the lounge with a towel around me. "Bonjour, how are you today?" was Henri's greeting as he stood in the doorway.

"I am good," was my reply.

"Bon! I would like you to pack clothes for four or five days and come with me. I would like to show you my French house and have you stay with me there," said Henri.

I was so excited and surprised by that offer, but sadly, I had to reject the offer. "I cannot come with you, Henri. I have no one to look after my doggy."

"I will be taking you and doggy, so pack what he needs. Pack clothes for yourself, and include an evening dress as we will be going to the local golf club dinner dance – that is, if you will accompany me," said Henri.

I rushed around, packing all the new clothes I had brought with me, sorting doggy's things, getting dressed, drying my hair, putting makeup on, and making sure I had my medication. I even packed nearly all my shoes, bags and jewellery. I glanced over to see what Henri was doing at this time. He was on the decking, smoking and admiring the views. Everything packed was in two small overnight bags. They were both full, very full, but all was correct. "Done." I shouted.

"Bon, then let us go!" he replied.

I turned off the water and the gas and locked the doors. With my crutch in one hand and doggy in the other and Henri with my bags, we got into the car and away we went. I phoned Ruth to tell her to help herself to the fresh food in the fridge and that I would see her later in the week.

I was so excited to be with Henri. I watched him as he was driving. He was older than me and very handsome. Oh, those eyes. As we drove, he placed his hand on my knee, and as we talked, he kept turning to look at me. Our eyes constantly met, electricity zapping me all over. "I am proud and excited at the prospect of showing you my house. It is quite something," he said. "I will attempt to make your stay with me most enjoyable."

He said the journey was less than an hour, but I presumed that was at his driving speed, which, to be honest, was a tad fast – well, very fast. On the way, he pointed out famous landmarks and asked me for my food likes and dislikes (I had none of the latter). We talked about tickle tackle, laughed, and flirted.

We reached a crossroads, where he said, "We are here. There, across from us, is my house." I was taken by surprise. I was expecting a small, beautiful French house, but there in front of me was a huge, red-bricked, Georgian house. It was surrounded by large conifer hedging with a large wooden entrance gate, and with his remote control, he opened the large gates and drove through.

"It is huge, Henri, not what I was expecting," I said.

"You have seen nothing yet. Prepare to be overwhelmed," he replied.

I needed Henri to help me out of these damned bucket seats, which he did and then held me so tight as he kissed me very lightly. "C'est bon," he said as he let me go.

The front of this large red bricked building had at least ten high Georgian windows, each at least twenty feet tall, with an entrance porch to the far right. To the left, the building it accommodated a large car park with no cars there at all.

The entrance porch had three large highly polished double wooden doors with Georgian mirrored top halves. Henri said to leave my bags, as someone would bring them later. "The first of these doors is to my music and recording studio, and I will show you that later. The second door is a private entrance to the living quarters, and the third is where I shall take you now. Prepare to be amazed!" At this, he opened the door and led me in with doggy. It was beautiful, a large, white marble entrance hall. It had white leather sofas in different positions, large lamps, trees in large containers, a circular marble and wooden staircase leading to the first f loor, and a gigantic crystal chandelier in the centre. To the left were six double doors, all with mirrored glass. Henri ignored those and took me directly across the entrance hall to a highly polished door and took me inside to what was a large living kitchen. A large wooden French table that seated at least ten was situated to one side. There were units all round – a three-unit solid fuel cooker, fridge freezer, washing machine, dishwasher, microwave, and coffee maker – in fact, everything one would need in a house this size. There were notice boards all over with children's paintings and pictures, photos, to-do lists, not to-do lists, leaf lets, restaurant menus, and more.

We continued through the kitchen to the outside rear door. It was a stable door with the top half open. I could feel the warm air blowing in. I followed Henri outside to where he had opened a small gate to a small grassy area with a kennel. There he was greeted with his little dog, a small golden King Charles spaniel or something similar. "Put doggy in there. Take his lead off, and let them play," he said."

"What if they don't like one another? Will they not fight?" I said.

"I have never known a bitch fight with a dog. They want fun and excitement, just as most bitches do. Do you agree?" he asked.

"I don't feel as if I have the right answer to that," I replied.

The whole of the outside of this side of the house had a large terrace with wrought iron fencing. There was a f lagged f loor with wrought iron garden chairs and tables covered with beautiful cushions. Large steps led down to the wooded and garden areas, at least thirty steps, where there were with large urns filled with f lowers on either side.

"Now that doggy is at home, it is time for you and me to have some breakfast. Come with me," he said, leading the way and holding my hand. Back into the kitchen and through to the marble hall where a woman in a blue uniform came forward. "Christine, my housekeeper, Silvie," he said. Silvie looked surprised and nodded, so I nodded back. Henri gave her instructions for breakfast, all in French. She agreed and made her exit.

Across the marble hall and bearing right to a large door, we entered the corridor that led to the middle entrance door. We turned right, and a few yards farther, he went through a door on the left side marked, "Guest Accommodation." I looked around this most beautiful area, what looked like an apartment, as Henri said "This is your accommodation, and if you like it, it will always be yours and for no one else's use."

As I entered this room, the first thing I noticed was the large windows with long, white cotton side curtains. On the outside of these windows was a large terrace with sun loungers, garden tables, and chairs, all with beautiful cushions. There were f lower pots and urns dotted around. On the inside of the window was a large white wooden dining table with six white chairs. There was a seating area with white leather sofas, coffee tables, a large television on one of the large walls, and numerous lamps on wooden f loors with thick woollen rugs.

To the left of where I was standing, I could see a huge bedroom on a raised f loor. There was huge bed with all white units on a dark wooden f loor with thick woollen rugs. Doors on the right of the bed showed the shower room with a bath and a walk-in wardrobe. All this area was partitioned off with a coloured glass brick wall that was curved to allow privacy to the bedroom area.

"This is beautiful, Henri! Did you design all this?" I said as I walked around and around.

"Yes, and I designed all the other rooms you have yet to see," came Henry's reply.

Just at that moment, Silvie arrived to set the large table with breakfast. There seemed an endless choice of various foods, far too much for two persons, but after Silvie left, we both sat and enjoyed the food and hot coffee. "When we have finished breakfast, put on your walking shoes. We are going on quite a long walk through part of my estate, ending at the most quaint small French restaurant for our lunch. I know you will love this," Henri said smiling and looking straight into my eyes. Oh, those eyes – they just keep zapping me with electricity.

"If I have your arm for support, then I need not bring my crutch," was my reply. To this, he nodded his agreement.

"If you are happy to stay here for a few days, I will arrange for someone to bring your belongings," Henri said.

"You will need to do that sooner rather than later, as I need my makeup and change of footwear now," I said, laughing.

"Done," he said. Within minutes, my bags were on the bed, ready to be unpacked.

"Leave them until we return," said Henri, and I freshened up, with new makeup and more perfume. "We will collect the dogs on the way out." With that, he held me tight and kissed me tenderly but seductively. I could not believe that this was actually happening to me, and I wondered if Henri was to share that bed with me at night. My knees and legs went weak at the thought.

After collecting the dogs and putting leads on them, we made our way down the large steps to the rear of the building and up the paths through the woods with me holding onto

Henri's arm. I could tell he was enjoying this, as he cuddled my arm into his. This felt very sexy and loveable, and I really enjoyed it.

Whilst we walked, we never stopped talking and laughing. We had so much in common it was unbelievable. We talked about family. He had a brother called Andre. There were only ten months between them. They were very close, shared everything, and did everything together as children. Now, Henri managed the band, and Andre managed all the finances and investments. Andre had a yacht and was away at present racing it in the American Cup somewhere in the Atlantic. I told him about my family, and I told him about what I did in business before I retired. The biggest revelation we shared was that two years previous, both Henri and I had lost our lifelong partners.

We sat on one of the benches we had found to rest for a while, and we continued to talk about our lost partners. I confessed to Henri that it was the loneliness that I found hard to cope with after my husband had died as well as the completely different lifestyle that had been forced upon me. Henri agreed to all that I was stating. He also felt lost and not in control. At this point, I could feel my tears starting. I tried so hard not to cry to no avail. Henri held me close, and he too was crying. We both cried and held each other tight for what seemed to be ages. "Come on now, Christine. Dry your eyes, and I will do the same. Let us continue mand have a good lunch. The dogs are fed up of waiting for us," he said.

We were now out of the woods and walking through pathed green fields. "From here, you can see the whole of the gardens, swimming pool, tennis courts, and band stage with outer buildings," he said, pointing me in the right direction.

"It is huge, Henri. You must have to have quite a number of staff to keep this large house running smoothly," I said.

"It is my pride and joy. Tomorrow morning, I have to work, so I want you to explore all the rooms you have not been shown. There are twelve bedroom suites. My bedroom is upstairs. Downstairs, there is a lounge, a gaming room with computer games for the children and of course for myself and Andre, my brother, and a pool room. Near the swimming pool is a building that houses a snooker room for the adults."

I was getting very tired at this point, and Henri noticed this. "Just there across the bridge, you can see the French bar and restaurant. Hold on to me, and we will safely arrive in style with two fantastic little four-legged friends." Sitting outside at a table with an umbrella open for shade, we ordered finger-type foods from shrimp to thin-cut steak and muscles to chips. We laughed, ate, drank, and kissed each other provocatively.

When we finished, I said, "Henri, I don't think I can make it back as quickly as when we came. I am so tired, and I will need to rest more."

"Do not worry, my beautiful Christine. I have ordered one of my cars to pick us up and take us home. How is that, madam?"

I laughed. "Brilliant, monsieur," I replied and kissed him again.

We arrived at the house. While Henri put doggies back into their pen, I made myself comfortable on the bed. I was so tired, as I was only a few weeks postop after yet another hip procedure. Henri remarked that I would be much more comfortable with no clothes on. I agreed, and he stripped off all his clothes. We both snuggled under the covers and had slow sex – and I mean very slow sex, a loving, relaxing sex that was fantastic. I just loved the feel of him, the taste of him, and the smell of him. I loved breathing his breath and feeling his lips and tongue on me. We both drifted into sleep.

I awoke to Henri jumping out of bed, getting dressed, and stating that he was going to the kitchen to prepare me an evening meal. It must have been about nine. I showered and dressed, and in no time at all, Henri was back with two hot plates of steak and mashed potatoes with a cream sauce over the potatoes. Henri said that this was his favourite meal, and therefore, it was to be mine. "Not very likely," I thought.

The next day, I woke to birds singing and the sun shining. Henri must have already left for work, so I got dressed. Silvie came in and prepared the table with all sorts of foods for my breakfast. I thanked her, and she left just as Henri popped in to say he would be back here at about one to have lunch with me. He had brought the doggies with him and suggested that I take the opportunity this morning to explore the rest of the house and the grounds including the swimming pool area. I agreed, and he left.

As Henri had instructed, I walked around the house with doggies in tow, starting with a large lounge. It was cream and brown with large sofas of brown leather placed at different angles in the room, a large television on the wall, coffee tables to each sofas, large lamps, and lovely rugs on dark wooden f loors. The large windows opened onto the terrace to the rear of the house. I walked onto the terrace and could see the stable door to the kitchen to my right. I returned to the lounge and then back into the hall where I continued through the set of large doors at the end of the hall. The doors all opened onto what could only be described as a ballroom. I walked across the dance f loor to the opposite side doors. I opened them to find an outside terrace that was an extension to the internal dance f loor. From this, you could see right up to the stage area, which was surrounded by lawn areas.

The doggies and I walked across the lawn areas and past the stage and buildings to the swimming pool at the rear. We sat on one of the poolside chairs and watched a pool man clean the pool. From there, we walked on past the tennis courts to the beautiful rose gardens. The f lower gardens were huge, and at stages, there were benches that the doggies and I took advantage of.

As the sun became hotter, we made our way back to the house, up the large steps through the stable door, and back into the hall. While there, I glanced into the doors to see what they were. It was nothing for me to get excited about – just gaming rooms of various sorts. I thought I would just have a quick look upstairs before I took advantage of a little me time before Henri came back at lunchtime. The first bedroom I looked in was, well, different, and it was obviously Henri's room. The whole of the ceiling was mirrored glass. It was a very large room with an en suite and walk-in wardrobe. I knew that Henri would entertain his women friends in here; the view above from the bed would be more than revealing and tantalising. I hurriedly left and returned to my quarters.

Silvie had left me coffee with hot milk. What a house-keeper she was! She seemed to know what you wanted before you knew yourself. It was then that I started to think about

Henri and other women. It was obvious that a man such as Henri would have some special women in his life – perhaps one special woman. Why was there no sign of a woman anywhere? It was reasonable to think that it could be that he was seeing a married woman and that is why there is no evidence of her. Perhaps he had just finished with a woman, or perhaps he just picked a woman when he wanted one for sex. He had many beautiful woman to choose from in his band. Why had he chosen me, a mature woman with no large boobs? I could not compete with any of the women I had seen around the music studio. I felt def lated. I thought it best to keep a look out for any woman who crossed Henri's path and might be interested in him.

Silvie brought us a hot lunch with strawberries and cream for dessert. Henri returned as he said he would, and we enjoyed lunch. "This afternoon," he said, "I am going to give you a tour of my music and recording studio." He was always excited to show me something different in his house. He asked me whether I had enjoyed my morning exploring his pride and joy. I replied that I loved it and so had the doggies. "I have told everyone to stay clear as I wanted the place empty for a VIP this afternoon," he said, laughing.

After lunch, we made our way into the music studio by way of the side door in the corridor my accommodation was on. No one there, and the place looked huge. Henri started to kiss and cuddle me as soon as we closed the door, and I got the impression that if I had allowed him to do so, he would have had sex with me over a desk or on the f loor or anywhere as he was so keen and aroused. I let him down gently by saying that

I really wanted to hear some of the new releases he had made first. A doorbell sounded, and Henri opened the door. Argumentative words were spoken and in walked the most beautiful woman I had seen in a long time. She was tall and fortyish with huge boobs and long auburn hair. She walked towards me, looking for something amongst the cushions and spoke to me politely in French. I replied with my most useful phrase. "Pardon moi. Je ne parle pas Français." With that, she found her purse and left.

We spent the afternoon watching and listening to all the new releases the band had been working on. It was only days before they all left for a three-month tour of New Zealand. Henri had been working so hard recently, and he said that after this coming tour, he intended to have a break for a few months.

It was late afternoon when we returned to my quarters. It was cuddles, sex, and rest in my bed for the remainder of the day. When we awoke, Henri said he would prepare me an evening meal. Guess what? Steak and mashed potatoes was the dish of the day.

The next day was pretty similar. After lunch, though, Henri, the doggies, and I drove to the coast where we walked the beaches, had ice cream, and stopped at a little beach bar for coffee and a brandy. We returned pretty late, but Silvie had not gone home, so she dished our evening meal out for us. Thank goodness it was a lamb casserole with crusty bread.

The next day was the day of the golf club dinner dance in the evening. We cuddled in bed and talked about it. Henri was to present all the winners with their prizes, and he said he was looking forward to it. Somewhere amongst the guests would be a woman – or perhaps women – who have been involved with Henri, so I would be watching. I asked Henri about the woman who came into the music studio the previous day. There was very little response from him, but he did say that he was angry that she had turned up after he had told everyone to stay away. The woman's name was Marcia. Someone to watch out for.

The next day at breakfast, Henri offered me some money and transport to purchase an evening dress for the dinner dance. I declined as I had brought a beautiful one with me. He told Silvie to assist me with anything I needed. If I wanted a hairdresser, Silvie could arrange it. Again, I declined the offer. With my short hair, there was no need of one. Henri was to work all day, but he would be ready for six-thirty, and I replied I would also be ready for then.

Today was only the fourth day I had been with Henri at his house. I knew now that he was a talented musician, a very wealthy man, and a businessman who owned and ran a successful band. He was a renowned song writer, and he owned many properties in France. All his wealth and finances were shared with his brother. Andre ran the property business and dealt with all the finances and investments.

I still could not understand why Henri found me attractive. I was a middle-aged widow and very plain looking, was slim with very short blond hair, had small breasts, and knew nothing about designer clothes. Why, when he was surrounded by beautiful women, had he chosen to go with me to this special evening at the golf club? Henri was to be the guest speaker and present all the prizes to the golfers for all the tournaments they had had over the last year.

Four days was all it had been. I really wanted Henri to be proud of me that evening, so I had to make every effort to look the part.

I had brought a long evening dress with me. It was made of knitted silk that felt like liquid. The colour was a pale green, but when it moved, it looked pale blue. It was magnificent, the colour dancing from blue to green and back. The dress had small capped sleeves, with the front going straight across just at the top of the bust line. It gathered in at the waist and then came out to f low gently down to the f loor. The back was high into the neck and gathered into the waist before falling gently to the f loor. I had brought some evening shoes that were more of a full boot-type shoe made in silver grey. They were fitted at the ankle with small leather f lowers with a two-inch heel. My evening bag was a box bag in crushed grey crystals.

I now needed Silvie's help, and I was a little dubious as to what response I would get. I had the impression that she was not happy about me being there with Henri. She had worked for him for many years and also for him and his wife before she died. I would say she was in her seventies, a good-looking woman who always looked smart. She ran the whole of Henri's estate, from the gardeners to the cleaners. She knew Henri's daily diary and always laid out the clothing Henri needed for the day. I needed her help with my dress attire.

I made a list of items I required to compliment my dress as well as some cosmetic items. They were tights with a silver sheen, elbow-length evening gloves in silver or light grey, black nail varnish, body gel with sparkles in it, and hair gel. All I had to do was ask Silvie. It must have looked quite comical, me playing charades with a list of items. To my surprise, Silvie smiled and showed she was enjoying the whole episode. She took the list, and after bringing me some coffee, she went off on her quest to bring me my requests.

The whole of that day was spent pampering myself. I sunbathed in the morning, had lunch and rested as much as possible, soaked in a perfumed bath, and washed my hair. Silvie returned with all the items on the list. The gloves she chose were really beautiful. Later in the afternoon, I covered my chest and back with the body gel that sparkled and painted my nails black. I was now ready to put the dress on and complete my transformation with face makeup, including silver and blue eye makeup, and my hair spiked at the back and feathered around my face. Jewellery was crystal earrings with matching crystal on a thin platinum chain worn as a choker. All was complete with the silver grey gloves worn with a bracelet over them. The bracelet was leather strands with crystals wrapped around the glove at wrist level. All was complete, and I was so sure I could not have done any better. I thought I looked brilliant. When Silvie brought me a snack and a hot drink, I could see from her reaction when she saw me in the evening dress that she was really impressed.

It was now time for Henri to come and collect me. It was six-thirty, and he was on time. I was really nervous as he entered the room, fully dressed in a dinner suit with a pleated blue shirt and bow tie. He looked so handsome and immaculately dressed, and I felt so proud that he was taking me with him. From the look on his face when he saw me, I was absolutely sure he was thrilled with what he saw. In fact, he was speechless for a few moments. He said, "Vous êtes une beaute."

(You are a beauty.)

Henri surprised me with a new a smartphone. It was encrusted with crystal chips and very beautiful, and I did not have the heart to tell him that I was much happier with my black phone that just did what it was supposed to do and nothing more. "A gift to thank you for your companionship over the past few days. I will transfer all your information on to it later," Henri said. "I would love to give you a ring, but I cannot, so I have bought you two rings. Come with me."

I held Henri's hand as we walked into the kitchen area. There were two men there, both jewellers, and they were there to fit me with large diamond earrings. Henri explained to me that these earrings were a special gift from him to me, but these earrings had to be fixed by these jewellers and were a permanent fix that only registered jewellers could remove. He explained that all the paperwork and insurance documents would be given to me when they had finished putting them in place. They were fantastic and certainly worth a fortune.

It was hard to thank Henri for these gifts. The earrings made my outfit look so designer and expensive. I looked and felt like royalty. We cuddled and took photos. Silvie was amazed at the presents I had been given and was happy to take photos of Henri and myself. "These photos will be for you to choose one for your screensaver on your new phone and remind you of me." Henri laughed.

When the two gentlemen had gone and Silvie had gone about her business, I caught Henri looking at me. I could tell he liked what he saw, and I looked at Henri and liked what I saw.

Henri's transport had arrived. I turned to Henri and

said, "I don't want to take my crutch. If you let me use your arm as before, I would feel better." He agreed and hugged me. I knew I would have to be so careful not to fall in love with Henri. He had made it so clear that after such a wonderful life with his wife died that he did not want any mushy love. That was why he said sex or fuck instead of making love. I also knew that there was a good chance that Henri was actually enjoying me in more ways than one.

We arrived at the golf club in style in a large white Mercedes, and we were escorted to the hall for the reception registration. Although everyone knew one another, it was the thing to do.

Henri registered us as "Monsieur Henri Chartress and partenaire Madam Christine Dalaney." I did not know that "partenaire" in French meant unmarried partner as in wife but not a wife.

We were escorted to the main entrance door to the ballroom and when our turn came, the official speaker announced us as "Monsieur Henri Chartress and partenaire Madam Christine Dalaney." At this point, I could sense a buzz of something around the ballroom, but at that time, I did not know what the fuss was about. I even watched as people congratulated us. We took our seats at our table, which was positioned next to the dance f loor.

Henri seemed to be busy with people all the time. At one point, an overweight gentleman asked me to dance. I looked to Henri to see what he thought, and he nodded his approval. After dancing with this Frenchman for several minutes, we were excused by a tall, good-looking man who introduced himself as John Preston, a local very wealthy farmer of the region. His words. At last, I found an English person. It was so good to have a conversation. He told me his wife and family were at the opposite table and that they would love an introduction to me, but I was sensible to refuse at this time. I was right to do so – when I mentioned it to Henri, he was not pleased that I had been dancing with another man without his permission, especially John Preston whom he disliked.

After a lovely meal, the biggest surprise of all came when Henri introduced his band to perform as the entertainment for the night. The curtain around the stage was pulled back to reveal the full band, and off they went. They performed brilliantly. All the while, Henri was walking back and forward conducting them and the lighting team. What a spectacle! I loved every minute of it. Once the band had finished and the curtain had closed, the time came for Henri to present the golfing trophies. Names were called, and each recipient went forward to receive his or her prize. The men shook Henri's hand, and the women kissed him on both cheeks, all but one woman, Marcia. She was Henri's golfing partner, and they won the prize together. When she received her prize, she kissed Henri, full on the lips, and not just for a few seconds. It seemed to me the kiss lasted for minutes.

I was jealous. This was the woman who Henri had told off for disturbing us in his music studio. I thought that there must be a woman or women in Henri's life. You can't be so good looking, sexy, and wealthy and not be caught by some good little woman somewhere. Why me? Was he using me to get revenge on another woman? Was he trying to make another woman jealous? All I knew was that the day after this dinner dance, I was to go back to my caravan. I did not know if I would see Henri again.

At the end of the evening, which had gone so well, Henri said he would meet me in the foyer. He rushed off to arrange our transport, but what he had forgotten was that I could not support myself enough to get to the top of the large staircase, so I remained seated until Henri realised that I had a problem. He never did. No Henri. At my deepest despair, John Preston turned up and gallantly gave me his arm. I made my way with John Preston to the foyer.

In the foyer, I found Henri talking with Marcia. Henri saw that I was holding onto John, and he was furious. I took Henri's arm for support, and at that point, he realised his mistake, but he still sulked and did not speak to me all the way back to the house. I tried to make conversation in the car, but he was having none of it. I told him why I was holding onto John and that it was his fault for just leaving me unescorted in a strange place, unable to support my weight and stranded. He was still having none of it. "So be it," I thought to myself. Why was he with Marcia again? Was he just using me? I felt upset and angry.

When we returned to the house, Henri helped me to my room and then went to his room to change. I was not sure if he would return to me or not, so I put my grannie nightie on and finished my packing for the morning. It must have been about an hour later that he came into my room. I was not going to be treated like that, even though I really liked him and I was so looking forward to having sex with him. I broke the silence by asking him how I was to return the earrings to him as I wanted nothing from him if I were to be treated so badly.

His reply was to strip me of my nightie, kiss me passionately, touch me all over, and pleasure me every way that he could. We both came together with so much sexual force that we could not let go of one another for quite a long time.

He told me he was away early in the morning, so transport had been arranged for me to return to my caravan. He was not one for texting or phoning, so if I wanted, I could sent him a smiley face from time to time to let him know I was thinking about him. He was to be away in New Zealand for about three months. He did not make any promises to me, and I did not ask for any. We both cuddled and fell asleep.

In the early hours of the morning, I woke to find Henri had gone. I could not sleep after that, so I finished my packing and prepared to leave.

Silvie brought breakfast, left, and later returned with the driver of my transport, who had instructions to collect my luggage. I followed him to his car, collecting doggy on the way and making goodbye gestures to Silvie. I made myself comfortable in the car with doggy, and we set off to northern Spain to my mobile home.

Once back at my mobile home, I relaxed and decided that I was not going to fret over Henri. It was what it was, so I had to forget him and get on with my life. Beth and my grandchildren were due to arrive in a few days for a week's holiday, so I put all my energy into preparing for them.

We had a brilliant time. The week went so quickly. With her Aunty Ruth and Uncle Matt, we went everywhere from beaches to Luna parks in the evening. In no time at all, it was time for them to leave. I would be joining them in England in a few weeks.

There was not one day that went by that I had not thought of Henri. I knew I was being extremely foolish. I was a middle-aged woman who had been f lattered by the attention of a wealthy Frenchman. I knew that I was not in love with him. It was in fact a sexual affair and nothing more, but I missed the excitement and the way he made me feel.

I returned to England, very pleased that I could drive it all the way without much difficulty. The days turned into weeks and then into a month. I sat one morning at my breakfast table, alone and bored. There was nothing different from before I met Henri. My routine was the same. Now and again, I would remember in great detail some of the times Henri and I shared. I would be strict with myself and stop all this nonsense, but it was hard. I missed him so much.

It was agreed that I was to be admitted back into hospital for further keyhole treatment on my hip. It was nearly two months since I had left Henri's house. I was drowsy with pain killers, and I woke from a nasty dream. I had also dreamt that I had spoken to Henri. It seemed so real, and I was so down and depressed that I decided to text Henri. I knew that it was foolish, but I really needed to. This is what I texted: "Think of me often, kindly and fondly, and do not forget me, Christine."

I knew as soon as I had sent it that it was the wrong thing to do. Within minutes, the reply came: "I kiss you." I replied, "I kiss you back."

I did not know what to think. I was sorry I had texted him, but I was pleased he had replied. Weeks went by, and on one Sunday morning, I answered the phone. "Hello, Christine. Henri here. How are you?"

"Hello, fine. How are you?" was my reply.

"I have a couple of months back in France before we start our Australian tour. Fancy keeping me company for a couple of weeks while I am working?"

"That would be great!" was my reply. I knew I should not have sounded so keen, but I was so excited.

"A week on Wednesday, I will send a car for you and doggy. Make sure doggy's passport is in order. The car will be with you at six that morning. You will be here by late afternoon. Phone me if there are any problems," said Henri.

"OK, no problem. See you then," was my reply.

"Looking forward to seeing and holding you," said Henri.

"Me too," was my reply.

Shocked and numbed, I sat there, not even being able to think. I went over every word he had said. Was this a good thing or a bad thing, me going back to that huge house? I was so excited that I threw caution to the wind.

I had just over a week to prepare myself for my visit to Henri's house: new clothes to buy, hairdresser to arrange, vets for doggy, sun creams to buy as it was the heat of summer, and more. Henri obviously knew I was in England. I presumed he must have called at my mobile home to find it all closed off.

The day finally arrived, and as arranged, a car was outside my bungalow bright and early. Doggy and I took to the back seat, and off we went via Le Shuttle. We slept most of the way and arrived by early evening. We parked at the side entrance, and the driver took my luggage. Silvie directed him to my room. I put doggy in the kennel area and followed Silvie to my room.

There seemed such a lot of activity in the house. When we passed the front of the house, I noticed that the front and side car parks were full. People were milling around outside through the dancing and band area. My attention was drawn to the plaque outside my quarters. It used to say Guest Accommodation. Now a new plaque in polished wood read Private followed by Christine's Room. Henri had always insisted that those rooms were never used for his women guests. Either he always had to find a woman called Christine or he would have to have other plaques ready for different women. I smiled at that idea, and I was secretly f lattered by that wooden plaque.

When I entered my room, I was shocked to find f lowers everywhere. New blue bedding adorned the bed, the windows were open, and the white linen curtains blew inwards. Memories came back to me of the four days I had spent there some four months ago. Silvie had disappeared, and my suitcases had been left in the walk-in wardrobe.

I did not want to mess about with any unpacking. I felt very nervous, so I thought it best to have a walk around the house. I went across the hall and into the kitchen and then outside to the back terrace. Nobody was around. I stood on the back terrace looking over the estate. I could just see the swimming pool behind the snooker building. I could see that Henri was there playing with two bikini-clad women. He was fully dressed, but he was grabbing these two women, at one point throwing one of them in the pool and holding the other over his shoulder. He was never short of female company and perhaps he was a sexual predator. I knew I was there to play with, but it was my choice.

I lost sight of them, and within minutes, Henri was stood at the kitchen doors. I smiled at him, and as he smiled back, he summoned me with his finger. I shook my head and summoned him to come to me. Oops. I knew he was going to set after me at a fast pace. I screamed with delight as he vaulted over a table and knocked two chairs over, grabbed me, spun me round, and kissed me. Talking through the kiss, he said, "I have missed you, I have missed you, I have missed you." The feeling of him holding me so close was what I had missed so much over the previous months.

"Welcome back, Christine. It is lovely to see you again," he said.

"Likewise, it is good to be back," I replied.

"We shall be eating out in about thirty minutes – Indian, I believe, if that is OK with you," said Henri.

"Yes. Will I be OK like this, or do you wish me to change my clothes?" I asked.

"You look fine. It will be a very informal, very relaxing meal. After all your travelling, I presume you won't want a late night. Did you notice the plaque?" asked Henri.

"Yes, brilliant, and I am f lattered," was my reply.

"You should be," laughed Henri.

I quickly refreshed myself, and within minutes, we were on our way to the Indian restaurant. When we arrived, we were shown to our table. At least ten people were sat at this round table. I was seated next to a woman on one side and one of Henri's employees – an accountant, I think – on the other. Henri was across the table from me.

I was so nervous, but I did not need to be. I met some great new friends that night. The woman to the left of me introduced herself as Trudie, wife of Andre, Henri's brother. She told me not to be nervous as she spoke good English and would translate all the conversations across the table. I liked her from the start, and she soon became one of my best friends and allies.

Trudie was a most beautiful woman, my age and obviously very wealthy. Andre was not going to join us as he was preparing his yacht for a trans-Atlantic race. As the night went on, she invited me to her estate to show me round and show me the stables and horses. We got on very well, and I found myself relaxing and being myself with her and the other dinner guests. Trudie made me laugh, and by all accounts, I made her laugh. Good starting point in any friendship.

At the table, every time I glanced at Henri, he was watching me intensely. His lovely smile and those eyes … oh, those eyes – I felt that they could look right through me touching my soul, sending electricity through all my body.

Not only did I find Trudie as a new acquaintance, but I met Henri's daughter Dee and her husband, Marcus. Dee invited me to her house for the following week and invited Trudie as well so all us girls could get to know one another.

The evening went so well, and I was pleased when it was time for us to leave. I wanted some time alone with Henri. In fact, I had been looking forward to that all night, and it was so obvious that all Henri wanted to do was to get me on my own and hold me, kiss me, and make love to me.

We had the most fantastic night together. Even Henri was surprised at how we were so good for one another in the bedroom, even better than the last time we were together.

When we awoke next morning, it was great to see him there by my side. One smile from me and one smile from him was all it needed to set us up for a great day.

I went to stay with Henri for two weeks but ended up staying for nearly two months. It was always varied from day to day. Henri worked most of the day, but he spent evenings and weekends with me. On one occasion, he was allowed to take me as a passenger on his flight training only to get permission to stop with me for four days in Majorca in a beautiful hotel. We enjoyed each other's company, so everything we did together was extra special. In Majorca, we did have his trained copilot with us for some of the time, but it was still good.

During this time, I returned to my mobile home in Spain and spent five days there. Ruth and Matt were thrilled. We went out together to the beaches and had some really good barbeques at night.

Henri used a transport company that provided elite car transportation. I was given a card with security numbers quoted on it. With one quick phone call, I would have a car there waiting for my instructions. This enabled me to go anywhere I wanted, and I took advantage of this as I did not want to be at that house for longer than I had to be.

The house was always busy, mostly with Henri's musicians. They were in the pool most days, so I tended to stay on my private terrace or walk the estate with the dogs. I did try to get out, with the help of one of the cars, as often as I could. I was making more friends and acquaintances as the weeks passed.

One really memorable day out was the day I went to visit Trudie at her estate. I had not met Andre as he was always away on his racing yacht.

I arranged for a car to pick me up and take me to Trudie's and back to the house later that day. What a place Trudie and Andre had. It was about fifteen minutes from Henri's house. Large wrought iron gates opening onto a long winding entrance road. The house was huge. It was magnificent.

Trudie met me at the door. A servant took my coat. I did not take my crutch as my leg was getting stronger by the day. Trudie delighted in showing me around the large Victorian mansion. Every room so tastefully decorated. There was a kitchen to die for, the many bedrooms were all superb, and there were at least two large lounges. We settled down in the lounge that had French windows opening onto the rear terrace. There were f lowers everywhere.

We settled down for refreshments, and we got on so well that I felt at ease all of the time. I think we had a lot in common because our conversations never stalled.

Trudie showed me an app to download onto my phone. It was a French-to-English and vice versa help guide. It was brilliant. You typed something in, a word or a sentence, and the translation would beep as if you had a call. When you listened to the result, it looked as if you were answering a call. You could also use it verbally. Trudie said that if I could use it most of the time, I would soon pick up reasonably good French. It was worth a try.

We talked about Henri and Andre. She told me that they were so different. She had been married to Andre for forty years and had known Henri all that time and more. They were extremely close. Most days, they spoke to one another or emailed one another when Andre was away. As children and young men, they shared everything, even girlfriends. Andre idolised his two sons and three grandchildren. She said Andre was a brilliant husband, and unlike Henri, Andre felt uneasy around women, so never caused her any problems.

I asked her to tell me all about Henri. She replied that it was much more fun if I had to find out what he was like. She laughed all the time. Henri had lost his wife a couple of years earlier. She was severely depressed, and although it was not suicide, she had made no attempt to get herself better. She had quite a few medical issues. Very sad, Trudie said, as Henri was devoted to her and their children, but Henri was a great musician and travelled the world building up his career. He also liked his women. Trudie said that at that moment in time, Henri was a very sought-after eligible bachelor, and I ought to keep him in check if I wanted to keep him.

The tour of the estate resumed with the horse stables. They were quite a ways from the house, but a good walk with Trudie's dogs was most enjoyable. The stables, like the house, were huge. I counted at least six horses in the surrounding fields and a couple in the stables. Andre was passionate about riding and his horses. He was also passionate about his boat. Trudie said she hated horses and hated boats more, so they did not share the same interests, but they were happy as they were. When he worked, he worked in the family business's office on the way into Paris. It was Andre's responsibility to provide all investments, and it was Henri's responsibility to manage the band. Henri and Andre worked hand in hand and had made a fortune.

When it was time for me to leave, Trudie invited me to go shopping with her the following week. She wanted to buy a complete outfit for the winter. I was thrilled to have been invited, and I offered to buy lunch that day. We had such a great day, and when I returned to the house, I felt quite refreshed.

When Henri returned to me in the evening, I suggested we walk through the woods with the dogs as it was such a hot sultry evening. He agreed. He was pleased that I was getting out and was more surprised to find that I enjoyed Trudie's company. We laughed about some of his and Andre's pranks when they were younger. It was so good, holding onto his arm, laughing with him, and f lirting with him until we were back on our own in my room.

We loved making love to each other. There was no effort – it was so easy and relaxed. Curling up with him at the end of the day was the best thing about my visit there. When he sat at the table doing his work, I loved to grab his head from behind and kiss him everywhere. He would really laugh giving chase. We would giggle like two demented persons. I knew I made him happy, and he made me happy too.

Time was running out for us. It was only a couple of weeks before the band set off on its Australian tour. They were to be away six months. With ten days to go, the dress rehearsal was arranged in the industrial building on a business estate nearby.

Henri asked me to attend this dress rehearsal, and I was pleased to do so, even though I would be on my own as I knew nobody with connections to the band. A day or so later, I would be leaving the house and returning home, a prospect I did not relish.

On the day of the dress rehearsal, a car picked me up and took me to the venue. Henri had been there since earlier in the day. I entered through the side door. It was packed. A stage was erected on one side, and many people were milling around. I stood centralised to the stage and far back of the building. Henri acknowledged me, so I relaxed a little. The music started, and Henri was back and forth, checking sounds and lights. The music was fantastic. The show was two hours of brilliant entertainment. I was so proud of him. At different times, he would come over to me and ask what I thought. On one occasion, he was so excited about what was happening on the stage that he actually kissed me so seductively I felt embarrassed.

I discreetly looked around the building. I saw Marcia, and she was watching Henri all the time. There were many women there – singers, dancers, musicians – and all of them were beautiful young women. I felt a lot older than the majority of them. I still wondered at the fact that I was the one who was with Henri, and I was so pleased that Henri kissed me in full view of everyone in that building.

At the end of the dress rehearsal, a large cheer sounded around the building. I presumed it had been a huge success.

Champagne was popping all around. Henri was in great demand. He was so proud of that show, and the band was all ready to take it to Australia.

Henri came over to me and told me they were all going into Paris for a wild night to celebrate completion of all their hard work. He wanted to know if I wanted to go with him, but he warned me that he intended to get very drunk. With that in mind, I declined and told him I would be at the house when he came home. A car was arranged for me, and I went back to the house.

A security person let me in the house and arranged for the security person at the rear of the house to let the two doggies in. Together with the two doggies, I made myself comfortable for the night. I had a bath and did some packing, as I knew there were only days left before I would be going home. I had been home at intervals, but when Henri was going to be away with his band, I would be at home all the time.

I was dozing at about two in the morning when my mobile started to bleep with incoming messages. At first glance, I saw they were from Henri. They were picture messages, but they were not from him because he was in all the photos in the picture messages. Every picture showed him having sex and performing sex acts with a woman. I could not make out who the woman was, but I had a pretty good idea who she was, perhaps because of the colour of her hair.

I did not know what to do about the picture messages. Was I to phone Henri and tell him about them and how upset they had made me or wait until the morning and confront him then? The unwritten rule on tour was what happens on tour stays on tour. Should these revealing photo messages comply to the same ruling? I had known Henri for only a few months. I had no authority to start chastising him, and I could not compete with these beautiful girls he knocked around with. With only a few days left with Henri before I set back home, I thought it might be best to forget that I had seen the photos. I felt as though my heart were breaking, but Henri might not have known that the messages had been taken and sent to me. I settled back down in bed and tried not to recall the woman who was performing with Henri in the messages.

It was not long before Henri entered my room. He was not amused. In fact, he looked pretty angry. "Have you something to say to me?" he snapped

"Such as?" I replied quietly.

"I ask you again. Do you have anything you want to say to me?" he shouted.

"I don't know what you want me to say," I replied quietly.

At this point, he was looking around the room. Soon, he caught sight of my phone. He pushed past me to retrieve it from the bedside cabinet, knocking me into the iron base of the large lamp. I felt pain in my wrist. I had taken quite a knock. "So you have seen these photos," he shouted. "You don't give a damn about me. All you are here for is what you can get. Well, get out of my house now! They didn't even bother you, did they?" After deleting the pictures, he threw the phone at me and stormed out.

It took me a few minutes to understand what the hell had happened. At first, I thought I should finish packing and leave. I should not be treated this way, so I should leave so as to show him that he could not treat me this way.

Then I thought that perhaps Marcia was with him in his room. Because of that thought, I decided that I would not leave until I had sorted the misunderstanding out.

I changed into pyjamas that would allow me to look decent as I ran upstairs to Henri's room. The door was ajar, and I could see in the darkened room that Henri was in bed alone. I climbed onto the bed, lay practically on him, and whispered everything that came into my head. "I am so sorry that I did not mention to you about the photo messages. I did not think you would know about them, and I have no authority to start nagging and chastising you about them. I felt heartbroken and hurt, and I still do. You are hurting now, and I am hurting now. I don't know how to put this right. Please talk to me. I do not want to leave here and you. Tell me what to do to make this better. I don't want you to send me away. I will miss you so much. How do I make this better?" A few minutes later, Henri lifted the blankets for me to climb under. I held him so tight and kissed and loved him. We were both in need of as much reassurance that each of us could give. Henri was holding on to me so tightly, and he was so upset when he saw my swollen hurt wrist.

"This will never happen again. I am so sorry. Whoever is responsible for the taking and sending of those photos is history. That person is finished and will never work for me again. This will never happen again. No one will separate us from now on, as we are to marry," he whispered. We both drifted asleep, as I sobbed through my chest and into my breath.

The next morning after making love, I returned to my room. Silvie had just set breakfast out and was disgusted with Henri when she realised that he had broken the lamp and hurt my wrist. I did not tell her; she had realised it for herself. When Henri walked in my room, she was shouting at him in French, and he was so meek and quiet. He told her in French that it would never happen again and that we were to marry.

We spent all morning having breakfast and talking. I did my best to explain to Henri how I felt about other women in his life. "I cannot compete with younger, beautiful women," I said. "Please never f launt them in my face. If you hurt me like that, I should just leave."

"I hear what you are saying, Christine. Let us forget this incident now. Get dressed. I am going to buy you an engagement ring, and we shall contact Father Michael to arrange a wedding date that is before we leave on the tour."

I was so excited and relieved. It was not the outcome I predicted, but Henri was so loving, and he was so excited at the prospect of me becoming his wife. I was extremely fond of Henri, and his lifestyle was so exciting, but I did not think I was head over heels in love with him. For now, though, what we had between was so good that it would do for both of us.

After arranging a private viewing at a prestige jewellers, Henri purchased a beautiful single square platinum diamond engagement ring. It did not need altering, so it was on my finger as soon as it was bought. With my wrist in bandages and a ring on my finger, we set off to meet Father Michael at the local Catholic Church.

Our initial excitement and expectations soon waved. Father Michael was so pleased for us, but a period of three weeks for the bands to be read as well as the receipt of the marriage license was needed, so it meant we could not marry before the commencement of the Australian tour. "Never mind, it cannot be helped. We shall marry when we all return from the tour in six months," laughed Henri. "I shall apply for the wedding license now, so we will be all set to go."

The last few days of my stay at the house were magical. I had all the attention from Henri I could ever wish for. We laughed, we made love, and we cuddled during the day and night. As usual, Henri gave me a lecture about contacting him while he was away. "If you need anything, contact me. Send me smiley faces to let me know you are OK and that you are thinking about me and missing me. If you want to use the house to entertain your family and friends, help yourself to whatever," Henri said. A car was sent for me and doggy, and true to form, Henri was not there to say goodbye. Nothing new there!

Six months was a long time. It would be February when they all returned. I returned home to my bungalow, and it was not long before everything was back to the way it was before I met Henri. I loved having the grandchildren, going for long walks with doggie, and doing the gardening and a little painting here and there. I would sit at night, thinking about Henri. He was such a charismatic man – handsome, very talented, and a wonderful lover. I loved to feel his arms around me, especially at night when we were on our own. To be honest, I knew that Henri had quite an appetite for women. I knew that while away on the Australian tour, he would have his pick of many women to play with. I also had my suspicion that Marcia shared his bed most nights, but I had no proof and could not accuse Henri of any wrong doing. What happens on tour stays on tour was the motto.

As December came, and Christmas was just around the corner. I felt quite lonely, and yes, I did miss Henri terribly. I had had a few small texts from him, nothing to excite me. I kept thinking about Marcia having Henri over Christmas while I was on my own at home. I knew that they were resting in one place over the Christmas holidays and wondered if I would feel comfortable joining them for Christmas or New Year. The answer to that would be no. I don't think the band and troupe would feel comfortable with me there either.

Late one night, feeling very sorry for myself, I texted Henri this message. "Henri, you can fix this. Please arrange for me and you to meet anywhere on route over the Christmas period. I will f ly to any destination of your choice and meet you there. I am really missing you, and I know I will miss you so much more over Christmas. I am lonely, and I need you. Please, Henri, you can do this for me."

A few hours later, I got a text from Henri telling me to check my email. To my amazement, there in my inbox were details of f lights to Dubai, leaving December 20 and returning December 27. All the details I required were there. I was so thankful, and I needed the reassurance that he still wanted me at any cost. Henri phoned and told me that he was excited at the prospect of spending some time with me. He was missing me – or so he said. A car was to pick me up from home, and a chaperone would be in the car to place me safely on the f light. At Dubai, a chaperone would meet me and take me to the hotel where I was to wait for Henri as his f lights would arrive at a later time. My heart was pounding while I was talking to Henri. We both laughed at our nervousness and apprehension about seeing one another; it seemed such a long time since we had held each other close, and it was something we were both looking forward to.

The time up to the departure date was spent shopping for new clothes, having my hair and nails done, and wrapping presents to leave for Beth and her family. It was not long before all was ready and the car arrived with a young woman chaperone to take me to the airport. Everything went to plan. Quite a few hours later, I was shown to our hotel room where Henri said I had to stay put until he arrived. He did not want me getting lost in a strange city.

That night, I curled up in the large bed and fell into a deep sleep. The next thing I remember was Henri kissing me. For hours, we stayed in that bed. We made love and made love, kissed and kissed, cuddled, laughed, and did it all over again. Those few days together were so fantastic. I had him all to myself and vice versa.

Over Christmas and the days before and after, I had felt so close to Henri. We had warm weather, good food and drink, long walks, good entertainment, dancing, and nightly firework displays. Henri was as happy and contented as I was. We discussed arranging for our wedding when the troupe returned in a couple of months.

Those few days did not last, and we said our goodbyes. Before long, I was back at home.

Back home, I busied myself with cleaning and decorating. I would daydream about Henri. As the weeks passed, I was on a countdown to seeing him again. I could hardly wait. When Henri phoned to say that the band was all back safely after a very successful tour, he asked that I leave going out to France for a week or so, thus giving them all time to complete all jobs that needed to be done. I agreed and booked my car to pick doggie and me up at a certain time and date.

At last, that time arrived. Doggie and I were picked up by a car, and in no time, we had arrived at the house. It was very quiet. The kitchen was quiet, and no Silvie was to be seen. Henri was also missing. I looked around the house and in the music studio. I walked out onto the rear terrace. I presumed Henri must have been in the stage building, so I collected the two dogs and walked with them across the lawn area into the rear building of the outdoor stage. The noises I heard were quite distinctive. Somebody was having sex – very audible sex. I knew I should have walked away, but I needed to know who was making all that noise.

I walked into the corridor and slowly opened the door to the rear of the stage. I stood there for what seemed to be several minutes, watching Henri and Marcia having sex. Marcia was practically naked, bent over a table with Henri behind her, his shorts around his ankles. They were both so engrossed in what they were doing. I watched, feeling sick and hurt. Henri's dog ran in. He must have thought she had got out of her pen as he made no effort to look around and carried on with what seemed to be true enjoyment for him. My dog ran in, and that did make Henri jump with recognition. He turned around to face me stood there. He pushed Marcia away and desperately tried to dress himself. At the same time, he started to say, "It is not what you … " He could not finish that sentence as it was what it was. "Sorry to interrupt," I said calmly. "Please carry on." With that, I slowly exited the room, calling to the dogs to come.

Anger, shock, hurt, and every other emotion I could think of were deep in my heart. I felt sick. I could still recall Henri's face as he was fucking Marcia over the table. There was no doubt that they were both really enjoying one another.

I walked up to the rear of the house over the lawn areas, through the kitchen, and into my rooms. Within minutes, I had phoned the car central control and asked the dispatcher to send my car back. I took my ring off and left it with my mobile phone for Henri. I quickly packed the majority of my things, grabbed doggie, and met the returning car at the front of the house.

After calling at the local vets for doggie's medicine and passport endorsement and stamp, I settled down for the journey back home.

Henri never tried to contact me. He never went to my mobile home to see me. He never came to my home in England to see me. I was broken. It took a long time for me to get over what had happened that day.

As the days turned into weeks and then months, I found myself pining for the comfort of Henri's arms. I found myself thinking more and more about the sex we both enjoyed. I had to keep convincing myself that Henri had wronged me once too often. Life got back to normal. I even had a couple of dates with male friends, which were never serious and never sexual.

CHAPTER 4

Reconciliation

A year on, it was March (Easter), and I was back at my mobile home in Spain. There had been some problems with the rural site, and Ruth and Matt had found a rural site in France that they convinced me would be more suited to all our needs.

One morning, I woke so early that I decided to drive, with the directions Ruth had given me, to find this new rural site in France. I thought it was a good idea, as I was not sleeping well and a change is as good as a rest. Off I went with doggie to have a look at this alternative site. I took the coastal route, but after a couple of hours, I was thoroughly lost and had not found the site. I gave up going around in circles and determined that the easiest way to return to my mobile home site was to head inland and pick up the France/ Spain motorway.

Lost and tired and still looking for motorway signs, I pulled up at a crossroads. To my horror, across the road was a very large red-brick building. It was Henri's house. I paused to catch my breath. Was I to call? There were no cars parked anywhere. Perhaps Henri and his band were all away on tour. I pulled across the road, turned into the side street, and parked at the side entrance. My heart was beating so loudly. I did not want to leave without at least having a little look around. I checked myself and convinced myself that I looked very smart and attractive, so if I did see anyone I knew, I would feel confident with the way I looked.

I took doggie out of the car, entered the side entrance path, and slowly walked towards the rear kitchen door. I entered through the open stable door and I called "Hello" softly. Silvie walked in through the hall door, and she and I both jumped.

"Mon dieu!" she shouted and started to embrace me so hard I could not breathe. In broken French, I had to find out if Henri was at home. If so, it would have been better to leave straight away. "Non, non," said Silvie, so I relaxed. I asked about Marcia, to which Silvie replied "matrimony!" For one awful moment, I thought she meant that Henri and Marcia had married. However, she did not mean that, and in broken French, she told me that Henri was on his own and that she thought he missed me.

I nervously laughed and was aware that someone was coming in through the hall door. There, in all his glory and looking very annoyed, was Henri.

"What the hell are you doing here?" he shouted. "Leave before I get you escorted off my property."

"Thanks, Henri," I retorted. "I thought you could show me some manners after all this time"

He repeated, "Leave before I get you escorted off my property." He then pushed past me and put his coat on. After collecting his dog, he made his way down the large steps and into the woods walk way. Silvie pushed me towards the door. With hand gestures, she told me to follow him with my doggie. This I did, but I could not keep up with him. I still had very little strength in my hip and leg, and I shouted to him to wait as I was having difficulty with the steps and the walkway. I stopped, unable to continue, and to my amazement, Henri came back for me.

Within minutes, the sky turned black, and hail and rain came showering down. Henri rushed us to the stone cottage shelter. I was soaked and cold. Henri completely ignored me and doggie.

Although we were silent, I could feel a tremendous sexual attraction between us. I tried to look into Henri's eyes, but he was having none of it. As he offered me his coat and I accepted, I looked into those beautiful eyes. Oh, those eyes, sending electricity zapping through my body. I tried to touch him, but he moved well away from me. His phone kept calling, and he seemed to be having deep conversations. All my feelings for him were awakened. He seemed to be calmer and asked me quite politely, "Why are you here?"

"I found myself lost, trying to locate the main motorway," I replied.

"Bloody rubbish," was Henri's response to that. He kept asking why I was there. It was pointless answering him with the truth since he certainly didn't accept it.

I found myself saying, "I have missed you." As Henri moved nearer to me, my heart was beating so loudly that I was sure he could hear it. I moved towards him, and I kissed him, ever so gingerly, and he responded by holding me tight. We held each other for a minute or so, and his phone rang again. He walked away, talking on his phone and ignoring me.

"Do you want to come back to me?" he said. "If you do, there will have to be some changes. You left me, and you broke me into pieces. I could not allow you to do that to me again."

I did not know how to respond to that. I broke him? How dare he not remember why.

"Father Michael will marry us at eight tonight, yes or no? I will not be asking you again," was Henri's ultimatum. Weary and wanting to feel him, kiss him, and make love to him, I whispered, "Yes." At that point, he handed me his phone. "Say hello," he said.

"Hello … oh … Father Michael. Yes, candles tonight instead of f lowers would be lovely. See you later," I said. I was in total shock and a little fretful.

"Loving you can wait until after we are married, so stop your tears. Come, we have a wedding to arrange," he said.

By the time we had run back to the kitchen, we were both soaking wet. He had already spoken to Silvie who was as fretful as I was. In broken English, she told me not to worry about wedding clothes. She would clean and spruce the clothes I had on, and with some accessories, I would look the perfect bride. Henri left, saying that he had a wedding to arrange and he would see me at seven that evening. Silvie was to see to me, and Henri suggested that rest be the order of the day as it was going to be a long night. Silvie took all my clothes; ran me a hot bath; and left me with hot coffee, brandy, and sandwiches. I sat there in my rooms, trying to make sense of it all. I even phoned my sister, who was in Spain, to tell her what was happening. She knew as Henri had phoned her and invited them to the church. He had completely taken over my life and future. Was that what I really wanted? Too late for regrets, so I might as well enjoy the ride.

By seven, I was dressed in my black skirt and a white blouse that Silvie had placed loosely over the skirt. She had found a beautiful diamante thick belt and buckle for around the waist, a small black pillbox hat with black netting at the front, and black lace wedding gloves. I had my black stockings and small black boot shoes. I wore my own watch and bracelet. With my hair washed and my makeup complete, I was really pleased with the look Silvie and I had pulled off.

Henri walked into my room. He had a white suit on with a black shirt, all of which complimented my black and white outfit. He was carrying f lowers for us all. My f lowers were attached to my right wrist. Henri's f lowers were for his lapel, but I was not sure where Silvie was to wear her f lowers. Henri was also carrying a small thin box. "You look stunning," he said. "This is my wedding present to you," he added. I took the box and opened it, and I was amazed to see a diamond choker necklace. The diamonds matched the diamond earrings he had given me. They looked beautiful and expensive. Henri fastened the choker around my neck, we brief ly kissed, and I nervously laughed at the unconventional wedding arrangements.

"Wedding rings?" I exclaimed.

"All taken care of," was Henri's answer.

The cars at the entrance to the house all had white and blue ribbons attached. We made our way to the church in Henri's car. Silvie and the other members of the staff followed in the other decorated cars.

"I am very nervous, Henri. You have completely taken me by surprise. How do you know that you and I are really ready for this?" I asked.

"I know you love me, and I seriously love and want you. I will not let you ever leave me again. To be married will make it so much harder for you to hurt me by leaving me," was Henri's answer.

It was nearly dark when we arrived at the church. Lit candles were everywhere. It looked magical. I could hear a band playing inside the church. Obviously, Henri had been busy phoning and rounding up his band of musicians. I was taken by surprise at the number of wedding guests in the church. Ruth and Martin were there, and I recognised most of the friends I had made in France. All of Henri's family was there. With the band and troupe, the church was full.

I was really nervous as Henri and I walked down the aisle. Father Michael was waiting at the altar to greet us. We exchanged vows and wedding rings (Henri had chosen them), and after being pronounced man and wife, Henri took my hand, held it high in the air, punched the air with it, and shouted, "Done it!" The whole church erupted into shouts and cheers. What an experience!

A photographer was busy snapping pictures. Henri hugged me all the time. We made our way back to the house, where caterers had done us so proud with a buffet fit for a most revered couple.

A party followed. There was music, dancing, drinking, and eating. A couple of hours into the reception, Henri said he would like to leave and start our honeymoon. I knew exactly what he meant. I had no objection to that. I wanted and needed to be on my own with him. He looked so handsome and sexy in his wedding clothes, but I wanted to hold him in the privacy of our own rooms. We sneaked out of the reception and met in my room.

At last, we were on our own. Henri had always been a brilliant lover, and that had not changed. I surprised myself at how I needed Henri sexually. It had been quite a while! We had a wonderful few hours, just making love and playing with one another. I didn't ever recall going to sleep that night, but we did.

The following morning, Silvie woke us by placing coffee and juices on the dining table. Henri showered and then so did I. As we sat at the table, both of us contented with how the wedding and everything else went, we laughed and cuddled and waited for our breakfast to come. Silvie came in, and Henri asked "Where is breakfast?"

"With your guests in the dining area in the ballroom!" was Silvie's sharp answer. Henri and I looked at one another. We had completely forgotten about any guests. We both laughed and rushed around to get ready for our appearance at breakfast.

That was the beginning to our married life. Henri spoilt me all the time. He ordered me a new car, medium sized so I could get around easier. I was able to drive myself to visit friends and go to scc Ruth and Martin at the rural site in Spain. I f lew back and forth to home in England. All my family and friends in England were happy for me. If I wanted a considerable amount of time in England, a car would drive doggie and me back.

A few months after the wedding, I started to notice a change in Henri's behaviour towards me. He was always gentle and loving, but he made no objection to anything I did or wanted. If I said I wanted to go home for a month or so, he made no objection. At one time, he would not have wanted me to do things like that and would have stated his dislike and objection. He never argued with me, but the worst thing that I did not like was that he started to stay away for a day or so, usually with the reason that he had to see other musicians or shows or that he had to go to meetings in Paris with record producers. How was I to know if that was the full truth?

The months went by. My new sister-in-law Trudie was a marvellous friend. I had missed her husband, Andre, yet again, as I was back home arranging and attending my granddaughter's christening. Trudie loved her life. She rarely spent time with her husband as he was a yacht fanatic and was always taking part in some trans-Atlantic race.

At breakfast one morning, Henri said, "I would like to watch you having sex with another man." At first, I thought he was joking, but I realised he was trying me out as to would I or would I not.

"Don't be ridiculous, Henri. Not a chance. Please do not go there again. I hope you were not serious." No comment from Henri.

A week or so later, again at breakfast, Henri approached the subject of a third person in our bed. He said he got very excited at the thought of watching me having sex with someone else. I told him that I was deeply upset at the thought of him wanting me to have sex with someone else. "That is the difference. I will be there all the time. It is not as if you had gone out or away with another man. I shall be there and in full control of the situation." That was Henri's reasoning. "I really want to be there and watch while someone has sex with you. I am very excited at the thought of this, and as my wife, you should want to excite us both more. Things are a bit boring at the moment, do you not think? "I was speechless. I realised then that he was really serious about the boredom he felt in our bedroom activities. I did not want our relationship to falter.

We were good together. The worst thing was Henri staying out most of the night, perhaps one night a fortnight, and I did not know if he was seeing another woman – or women. I hated the house, I hated my life there, and I was spending more and more time at home in England. I knew I had to confront Henri with my fears for our future together. He was always so busy and never seemed to have much time for me. We still had a loving relationship, and our sex life was still very good, but obviously, it was not enough for Henri and definitely not enough for me.

Together, we attended many dinner parties, on an average, once a week. He was always attentive and loving to me, so I thought I would tell him how unhappy I was at the house.

"So you are quite happy with me but not living here at the house," was his first response.

"I am lonely, Henri. On the nights you do not come home, I imagine you are with another woman. I sit alone, and I have no one here. I am so unhappy and lonely. I need a home, not a house. I need a home for you to come home to me. I know our relationship would prosper if I were to have my own house, a log burner in a lounge, a beautiful kitchen, my kitchen, where I could prepare our meals, and a beautiful bedroom we could cuddle in at night. You could go to work at the house from there, and I could be in a position to invite friends over for coffee or a meal. I could have my family, especially my grandchildren, stay with me in bedrooms next to mine," I said quietly and calmly.

"It is not the time yet for us to change things so dramatically," replied Henri.

"I will retire soon enough – if not retire, maybe semi-retire. Then we will have a place of our own that will suit both our requirements. Until then, can we try to be patient? I do not like change. If you are so unhappy, why don't you go back home more often?"

"Fine," I shouted. We cuddled in bed that night with not one mention of the conversation we had had.

A few days later, Henri presented me with computer printouts of properties for sale, all within approximately seventy miles from the house. "Have a good read. Choose three properties you would like to view, and I will arrange viewings for next Sunday. I am not promising anything, but I just want you to see what could be available. When Andre is back, he has over a hundred properties that we rent out. Perhaps he might be the one to help us with our search when the time is right!"

Sunday came, with viewings arranged for three properties, one at eleven, one at one, and one at three. All the properties had six, seven, or eight bedrooms. All had four reception rooms and large kitchens and dining rooms, and all had large areas of land with swimming pools.

We viewed the three chosen. What a disappointment they all were. Trying not to compare them with Henri's estate was impossible. Nothing was going to get Henri's attention, nor mine for that matter. Henri turned the car around to make our way back when I noticed a small for sale sign at the end of a long drive. The gates to the drive were open, and I begged

Henri to drive up to the house in the distance.

Henri was not pleased, but he turned into the drive and drove to the front of a beautiful Georgian mansion. It was all stone with pillars at the front door.

"You can't just knock at the door and ask to see inside," objected Henri.

"I am going to try," I replied. I knocked, and an old gentleman appeared at the door. We apologised for our untimely appearance, but the gentleman said his wife would be pleased to have us view the house.

From the moment we drove down the drive, I was in love with that house. The inside did not disappoint either. There was wood panelling everywhere, seven bedrooms all requiring en suites, and no central heating, and it required a new kitchen and main bathroom. It would require a considerable amount of work and money, but I could see the result being spectacular. I would finish it off with landscaped gardens and a swimming pool. All the stables and stable block would be revamped.

We thanked our hosts for their time and hospitality, and Henri and I made our way back to his house. Henri agreed with my vision for that old house. "I will make some enquiries, but I am not promising anything. It is not the right time for us, but I agree that if it was our right time, that house would be perfect," he exclaimed.

"Job done," I thought to myself.

Henri never mentioned that house again, but I did. He avoided committing to such a large project, so I lived in hope that he would change his mind.

The following weekend, Henri was holding an open

day party for all. It was to mark the release of the band's latest long-playing CD that was already proving to be a great success. Silvie was magnificent at getting caterers in to do these large functions. Although Henri always insisted that I was the lady of the house, I never did anything at all. I left Silvie in full charge of everything.

The open day party day came. Henri was all excited, and we both greeted the guests as they arrived. The day went really well. Children were everywhere. There was loud music, dancing, games, a massive food buffet, and loads of drink. As the day turned into evening, most of the families had left, and I played hostess by seating at various tables and chatting to everyone. Most of the men including Henri had
= disappeared, presumably playing poker or snooker. I was not drinking, but I took a glass of punch and really enjoyed it. I decided to have one more glass of the punch and then slip away to my rooms for a relaxing night.

I finished the second glass, and as I stood to make my way to my rooms, I began to feel the effects of the punch. I started to feel drunk. I made my way as quickly as I could to my rooms. By the time I got there, the rooms were spinning around. I felt really sick. As I fell to the f loor, I was sick everywhere. I could not stand up. In fact, I could not lift my head up as the rooms spun and spun. I was panicking as I did not know what the hell I could do or who I could get to help me. I was completely helpless. I was sick again as I lay there on the f loor.

I don't know if I lost consciousness, but I heard Silvie talking to me. "Don't worry, Christine. I am here now, and I will see to you. You have just had too much to drink. Let me just clean you up and put you to bed. You will be fine in the morning." I could not even talk. I tried to thank her as she took my clothes off and washed my face. As I lay in the bed with the room spinning and spinning and sick in my nose and mouth, I knew she was cleaning the dirty f loor where I had been. I was so embarrassed. I had never been that drunk before, even as a teenager. Silvie placed a large towel at the side of the bed and told me to be sick on that rather than on the bed. I grunted agreement.

"Try to sleep it off," said Silvie. I did not dare open my eyes as the spinning motion caused me to feel extremely sick. I hoped sleep would come to me quickly.

I must have fallen asleep as the next thing I remembered was that Henri was talking to me, whispering to me, telling me not to worry as he was there. He was lay across my shoulders and neck. I could not move anyway, but with Henri laying that way, it was impossible for me to move. "You are OK, I am with you all the time," Henri said.

I sensed a presence of another person in my darkened room. I tried to tell Henri that I thought there was someone else there, but I still could not get my words out. Henri tightened his hold across my shoulders, his face directly in front of mine. I felt this third person on my bed, and I knew exactly what was about to happen. "Just relax, Christine. Are you sure you are all right with this?" asked Henri. I could not answer, I could not speak, and I could not even lift my head off the bed. The room was still spinning, and I felt extremely sick.

My legs were gently moved, and I felt hands stroking my legs from my feet to the top. They stroking me across my stomach and my breasts. "You are OK. I am with you. Just relax and enjoy this," whispered Henri.

I was not afraid. I was angrier that Henri had arranged this, even though I had repeatedly rejected his request of a third person in our bed.

As I felt this person having sex with me, I was ashamed to find that I really was enjoying it. I had no control over what I was feeling. The more he caressed me and made love to me, the more I was aroused. Henri moved for a few seconds, and I found myself looking directly into the eyes of this person. Henri resumed his position, and it was not long before I climaxed. It was a very powerful orgasm. I even felt this person's ejaculation, something I had never felt before.

It was all over so quickly. In my darkened room, I was on my own again. I was sick on the towel, and I drifted off into a drunken sleep again.

At last, I woke to the dawn. I was feeling sober but very hung over and shaky. At first, I was not sure if I had dreamt up the incident. I made my way to the bathroom very gingerly and showered for a long time. After dressing, drying my hair, and putting some makeup on, I stripped the bed of all bedding, even pillows. The mattress was dry and clean, thank goodness. Otherwise, I would have discarded that as well.

I made my way to the kitchen and told Silvie to collect all the discarded bedding, destroy it, and replace with new clean bedding, even the pillows. From there, I collected the dogs and slowly walked up to the woods.

I sat for a while on a stone bench. I could not believe that Henri had done what he had done to me. I decided that I would leave and go home for a while. I felt so guilty that I had climaxed. How could anyone have an orgasm while being abused?

As I made my way back to the house, I could hear Silvie shouting for me. She had sent one of the ground staff to find me. In broken English, she told me that their doctor was on his way to see me. Someone had poisoned the punch at the party with something alcohol-based, maybe antifreeze, and that I was not the only one poisoned. A few guests had been taken to hospital. There had been no fatalities, but it was obvious that I was pretty poorly during the night.

The doctor took blood tests to check on any damage I might have caused myself, and a local nurse was brought in to administer intravenous f luid drips, of which I received about eight. Henri was beside himself with worry. He was so upset that he did not know that I was in real danger that night. He did wonder why I had not objected to what was happening and why I had seemed to enjoy it.

I was too weak to argue my case. I arranged to go home to recuperate and was relieved when I was finally in my own home with doggie. I had told Henri that I would never forgive him. I was seriously considering not returning to France and the house at all.

A few weeks later, Henri had never been off the phone trying to persuade me to come back to him. His daughter phoned and asked me to be godmother to her lovely baby girl. I couldn't say no, so I arranged to return to the house for the christening the following week. Henri promised to make it up to me. He had missed me so much.

CHAPTER 5

Meeting of the Brother

The day arrived for the car to collect me and take me and doggie back to France and the house. I had purchased a beautiful outfit and accessories for the christening.

When we arrived at the house, I was greeted by so many of the staff and band members, but I still felt hatred for Henri and that house. I looked so pale, but I was feeling more like myself. I let Henri love me and decided to try to put all the bad memories behind me.

The day of the christening arrived. Henri and I arrived at the church with plenty of time to spare. I walked amongst the guests on the grounds of the church, talking to most of them. It was a lovely sunny day, and I was feeling much better. Silvie had arranged for the caterers to set up the christening buffet while we were all at the church, so all I had to do was relax and enjoy the day.

The baby, in all her refinement, was being held by a man standing near the church entrance steps. I walked over to them and admired the beautiful outfit the baby was wearing, and I looked up into the eyes of this man. Shocked at what I recognised, I knew he was the man who had abused me that fateful night. I must have f linched or made some gesture that showed my recognition of this person, for he acted quite awkwardly towards me, gave me the baby, nodded, and walked away.

81

I was shocked and felt quite sick and disgusted. It was only when I calmed myself down that I realised who he was. There was a small likeness to Henri, and I knew it was Andre, his brother. I should have known, as Henri would never have let anyone touch me, but when it came to his brother, I had heard stories that they had in the past, especially when they were younger, shared girlfriends or women. I had been told so many times that they were so close, that they shared everything, and that they were inseparable. I had never met him before that day.

The photographer was shouting for the godparents and child. Andre came and stood beside me. He was the godfather! "Could the godfather place an arm around the godmother, and both of you look down at the child?" said the photographer.

"Pleased to meet you at last, Christine," whispered Andre. "It would be prudent not to tell Henri of your recognition. It would be bad for both you and me," he whispered again.

As we posed for the christening photographs, I was so aware of us touching each other closely, and I was very embarrassed to be aware of a strong attraction to Andre. We even held hands at the font in the church. I was so relieved when it was all over and Henri and I got in our car and made our way back to the house for the christening party. I did not mention to Henri anything about Andre, only that at last we had met. "You will adore Andre, just as I do," said Henri.

Back at the house, I took up my position as the lady of the house, greeting all the guests and overseeing that all the arrangements were as they should be. So many children were there. There was laughter, music, dancing, and games; the buffet was spectacular; and the atmosphere was wonderful. The poor baby was being passed from one person to another, as is common at christenings. I made myself comfortable at one of the small tables, and I watched all the children dancing.

I watched Andre on the stage sorting music and music videos out for the teenagers. He was taller than Henri. There was a slight resemblance to Henri, and he looked a little older than Henri. Andre was very handsome with a good physique for his age, with dark hair highlighted with silver. From what I had been told, Andre loved his horses and his yacht and adored his grandchildren. He was married to my close friend and sister-in-law Trudie, and they had a very large estate with farmland and stables on the way towards Paris.

When I had visited Trudie at their estate, she told me that Andre was nothing like Henri. He was a quiet, thoughtful man who liked the quiet life, but he had a passion for breeding and racing his horses. Andre was also away from home a considerable amount of time. After what I now knew about him, was I really to believe he was this saintlike husband, father, and grandfather?

Having found out that he was the person who had been in my bed and had had sex with me in front of Henri, I was surprised to feel calmer about the incident. My fear was heightened by the fact that I did not know the person and that one day I could be subjected to something worse. Knowing that Andre would never cause me any ill fate and the fact that I knew it was Andre made me feel so much better and some of my fears disappeared. How was I to face him? I was disgusted, embarrassed, and truly at a loss at how to act when with him.

The older children were upset that Andre could not get the dancing videos playing from the iPad to the large screen on the stage and came to me to ask if I had a lead that would work. I returned to my rooms with at least six older children, and between us, we riff led through drawers and cupboards in search of the required lead. Andre followed us into my rooms and insisted that he would find one if there was one to find. As I sat on the f loor with open drawers around me, Andre found what they needed. The children ran out screaming with delight.

Awkward! Andre started to leave, thanking me for my help. I nodded in agreement. "Can you get up from there?" Andre asked.

"Err. Perhaps not without some help," I answered smiling. The feeling of him holding me around my waist and pulling me up towards him was so exciting. It was so pleasant. I could feel my heart beating so loudly. I could feel his breath against my face as he helped me stand and get my balance. "Thanks, I did not fancy being stuck there all night," I said, trying to make a joke of it. He smiled and left.

From that encounter with Andre, I could never watch him, look at him, or stand close to him without that delicious feeling ripping through me. How could I? I even found myself daydreaming about him.

As the christening day came to a close, families were leaving, and I played the dutiful hostess, thanking guests for coming as they left. Henri, Andre, Trudie, and other family members and close friends made themselves at home in the large lounge. Henri and Andre were drinking and laughing. It had been a wonderful day. I arranged with Silvie that in a little while, she could serve some hot food to us all.

As the night progressed, I was so aware that Andre was watching me as much as I was watching him. You could say that it might have been misinterpreted as f lirting. So what? What I was feeling was so different to feelings that I had for Henri? When the guests started to leave, I had the pleasure of feeling Andre's lips touching mine as he said his thanks and goodbyes. So pleasurable, so exciting. That night, as I fell asleep, I wondered if Andre felt any of what I was feeling.

It must have been about a week or so later that our paths crossed again. Trudie had invited me over to the estate for a light lunch and then we were to go to the shopping mall. Henri gave me a lift there, and as I entered the house by the side entrance, I was all excited, hoping that Andre might have been somewhere around.

"I told Andre you were coming here today," Trudie said, "He wants you to go to the stables as he has something to show you. You will be surprised, and you will love it," laughed Trudie. I told Trudie I would go to the stables later, but she insisted that Andre was waiting for me.

I walked the pathway from the house to the stables, feeling quite sickly and excited. I wondered what the surprise could be. Trudie would not even give me a clue.

I entered the stable yard to find a couple of stable girls there and inquired as to where Andre would be. "In the stable block at the end of the yard," was the answer I received. I made my way down the yard as Andre came out of a building. "Bon, it is good to see you belle soeur," smiled Andre.

"What is this big secret I have to see?" I asked.

"Come, you will have to be very quiet. No sudden

movements please," was Andre's response.

Holding my hand, he led me into the end stable block. At the end stable in that block, he stopped. Facing me into the stable, he placed one of his hands to the left of me onto the stable gate and his other hand to the right of me onto the stable gate. I could feel him leaning against my back, and I am sure that he must have been able to feel my heart pounding. "There, what do you think of those?" I was so disoriented that it took me a minute or so to realise what I was being shown. There was a large mother horse with two small beautiful foals next to her. That was a great feel-good factor by any count.

"They are gorgeous," I whispered.

"Shhh," Andre said.

I turned to my left to whisper a question as Andre was bending down at that side, and it was inevitable that our lips would meet. A small kiss happened, only for a brief moment, but all the feelings were there. Holding my hand, Andre then led me out of the stable block and into the yard.

"They are beautiful. When were they born?" I asked.

"The other night. They are a little too small at the moment, but they are good and strong, and they have a really good mother," replied Andre.

"Sorry about before," I said with reference to the kiss.

"Why? We have done a lot worse than that!" Andre said mockingly. I was mortified. It was still a raw and embarrassing episode to me. How could he treat it so f lippantly? I turned to walk away as I could feel tears in my eyes. "Wait! Where are you going? I will drive you round to the house," Andre shouted.

"No, I would prefer to walk, thank you," came my reply. As I neared the house, I contacted the car office and asked the dispatcher to send me a car as soon as possible. I then made my apologies to Trudie, stating I felt a little under the weather and that I had ordered myself a car.

It was not long before Trudie said that my car had arrived. I made my way to the front of the drive via the side entrance, only to find that Andre had arrived there and was in the process of sending my car back.

"What are you doing?" I asked him.

"Get in my car. I think we need to talk," replied Andre.

"Why did you send the car away?" I repeated.

"Get in my car; I think we need to talk," he repeated.

I was feeling quite fretful, and it was taking all of my concentration to stop myself from breaking down, so I got into the passenger seat of Andre's car. Andre got in, and we drove away.

As we drove towards the coast, Andre said, "I thought we were OK. Obviously not. Talk to me. What am I missing here?"

Trying not to cry, I said very quietly, "The memory of that night is still raw and very uncomfortable for me. I knew what was happening. I did not know, why, who, or why Henri was prepared to put me through that. I felt that I was being …"

"No, no don't you even go there," shouted Andre. "You did not make any effort to say no, and I know you enjoyed it as much as I did. I felt it in you!"

"I could not even lift my head off the bed – never mind trying to speak. I had previously said no to the idea when Henri had mentioned the possibility of it happening. How could he have done this to me? I was so ill with the poisoning, and the thought of not knowing who the third person was in my bed has made it a frightening experience for me." I cried.

We arrived on the beach front, and Andre parked. I was still crying a little. "Stop your crying now!" ordered Andre. "I was not aware that you had made it clear you wanted no part of it. I saw no reason to stop. There was no sign of distress from you. I had no intention of hurting you, and I really thought that we both shared the experience and enjoyment. Sadly, I was wrong. Tell me: Did you not enjoy me? "Andre asked.

"I really enjoyed you and knowing now it was you has made it easier for me to be less fearful," was my reply.

From the boot of the car, Andre brought two neon orange-and-silver padded yacht jackets. One was for me, and the other was for himself. "These will keep us warm as we walk the beach," Andre said. He offered me his arm, which I gladly took and wrapped myself round his side. It was close and cuddly, warm and secure. I also felt the strong physical attraction to Andre that I had felt before.

As we walked along the beach, we talked, laughed, joked, and held onto each other so closely. "Are we OK now?" asked Andre. "Where do we go from here? Are we just good friends, or maybe close friends, or very close in-laws? Do you want me to leave you alone?" he said.

"I think we make a splendid brother-in-law and sister-in-law. Close and loving, I think we should be."

"Bon, does that mean I can get up close to you and try sexually motivated kissing?" remarked Andre, and we both laughed.

"In England, we have a saying about being kissing cousins. It means heavy sexual petting allowed, but that is it,"

I said, and both of us laughed.

We turned and walked back to the car, stopping in the stone promenade shelter to rest from the cold wind. It was not long before Andre had his arms inside my coat, and I had my arms inside his coat. As Andre pulled me towards him, he said, "Hold me close and closer still." We were so close I could feel his heart beating. I could feel his body pushed up against mine. We kissed and kissed, and the feelings were as great as if we were having sex. "No, we must go now," said Andre. "I really love Henri. We have always been very close. We have done everything together through all of our lives. Neither of us could function without the other. I would never hurt him. I would never cross that line. You are that line, Christine," he said quietly, making sure I understood what he was trying to say. "So kissing cousins we are," he added, and we both laughed and cuddled together.

As we returned to the house, Andre said, "I shall ask Henri for his permission to take you to my yacht next week. We have to take her out of the harbour to test the engine pressures. It is a trip of around four hours. Are you OK with water, cold, and speed? Do you get seasick?"

"Yes, yes, that sounds brilliant. I shall really look forward to it," I replied.

That night, I was excited at what had happened with Andre earlier that day. I kept thinking about everything he said and did. Thrills ran up and down me as I closed my eyes to remember those sensuous kisses. Henri said that he had no objection to me going on the yacht with Andre and his crew. I could not wait for that day to come.

It was not long before Henri got the call from Andre to

say that the day after, the weather conditions were favourable, so he would collect me at eleven.

Dressed in dark blue jeans, a white sweater, and white trainers, I waited patiently for Andre to collect me that morning. When he arrived, he gave me a new white yacht jacket and a white yacht cap, both with the yacht emblem printed on them. I was so excited when he entered my rooms that I felt uncomfortable and embarrassed, and I knew my face looked all f lushed. At my age, how could I find myself feeling like this? I knew I was falling in love with my husband's brother.

As we set off towards the harbour, Andre said, "I have been looking forward to seeing you again. I hope you will enjoy spending today with me and my crew. If you feel seasick, do not worry about it. It will pass. If it does not, we have a few toilets for you to use," he said laughingly.

As we parked on the harbour front, Andre pointed and said "What do you think of her?" He seemed to be pointing at a huge boat that looked like a mini cruiser.

"That one there?" I asked.

"Yes, that one," was his reply.

"I thought you said she was a yacht?" I asked, a little confused.

"She is a beauty of a yacht. You obviously cannot see her with her sails out, but when she is in full rigging, she doubles in size. Quite spectacular; speed no barrier!!" Andre answered.

On board, I was introduced to four of the crew members – one English man, Dave, and three Frenchmen, Marcus, Tony, and Jon. The other crew member turned out to be a French woman called Susan. Today, this woman was not on the yacht. I would have really liked to have seen her. While they were warming the engines, Andre gave me a tour of the yacht. The lower deck was primarily for crew quarters. The next f loor housed the lounge with a television bar area, a fully equipped kitchen, two double bedrooms with small en suites, two single bedrooms, and a large shower and toilet room. Along the small corridors there were pictures on the walls. Some showed photos of the presentations the crew had received from successful races, some showed pictures of places they had been, and some of them showed pictures of all the crew members. I could see what Susan looked like. I was not amused. I would say she was about forty years old with long dark hair. She was slim and fit, and she was a very good looking woman.

"Tell me about Susan," I asked Andre.

"Not much to tell. She is a great sailor and is great for morale," was his answer. Something told me that this Susan must have shared Andre's bed, but I could not ask that question. "Come up to the top deck and the navigation room; we are leaving in a few more minutes" Andre said.

The navigation room was filled to the brim with computers, charts, maps, and all technical machines and printers. The crew, including Andre, had Bluetooth ear- and mouthpieces. I was put into a lifejacket and strapped into one of the chairs. Off we went.

What a fantastic afternoon we had. At one time, I was unstrapped from my chair standing at the helm with Andre holding me from behind, so closely I could feel his excitement. I could feel his breath on my cheeks. We laughed as we tried to keep our balance as the yacht went, up, down, round, and sideways, heaving back and forth.

Before long, we were coasting back into the harbour. "Well, how did I do? No seasickness and surprisingly no fear."

"Wow, I thought that was exhilarating." I said.

"You did brilliantly, and I am glad you enjoyed it," answered Andre.

It took quite a while for the yacht to be moored, so I waited in the kitchen/lounge area for Andre to collect me and take me back to the house. When he came down the steps to collect me, he said that we were alone as the others had rushed off. He poured me a brandy and set the coffee machine off. I was hoping that he would try to seduce me or at least take some sexual liberty with me, but he was the perfect gentleman. We talked and laughed, and I knew that he wanted me just as much as I wanted him.

"Will Trudie not mind that you have brought me on the yacht today?" I asked.

"Why should she?" he replied. "I love Trudie to death as my wife, but we are not lovers. We have not been intimate for many years, but I would not let on to Trudie that I have said those things about us. She is always showing me off as the perfect husband to all her friends, and she would be mortified to find out that you know something different. When are you going back home to England?" Andre said.

"I don't know. I am not in as much hurry to go back this time," was my answer.

"Why?" That was the question, and the answer was that I looked forward to Andre more than I was looking forward to going home. "Why?" he repeated the question. I could feel myself blushing. A woman of my age desperate to feel some sexual contact from this man – how could I be so stupid?

"You will probably not like the answer," I said.

"Try me!" Andre said.

"Well, I know we kissed and cuddled and joked about kissing cousins but …" I stopped as I was not sure how to say what I was feeling.

"But what?" Andre prompted me, and at the same time, he moved very close to me. He placed his hands under my sweater; stroked my breasts, stomach, and hips; and pulled me close onto his face and mouth. There was no denial that we were extremely attracted to each other, and I wondered if Andre really would stop our actions before it was too late.

That evening on the yacht, there was no sexual intercourse, but there was an awful lot of sexual contact. Very, very heavy sexual contact. It was so much so that we both found it so easy to gratify each other's sexual desires. For a while, we held each other so close and so lovingly. "Well, belle soeur, I think we had better get you back to the house before Henri sends a search party." Andre whispered, "I have really, really enjoyed our time alone together, and I do not want you to disappear back to England yet. After enjoying every minute with you here, I would like to know that you and I could keep doing this until we tire of one another. What do you think?" asked Andre.

"I will never tire of you, Andre. I am truly besotted with you, and I don't even feel guilty. Is that wrong?" I said quietly.

"No, it cannot be wrong if we both feel the same and we do not cross the line," Andre answered.

Andre returned me to the house, and before leaving, he asked if he could pick me up and take me to lunch one day. "I would really like that," I said.

"I will ask your husband's permission first," said Andre with a laugh.

A few days later, Henri said that Andre was to pick me up at eleven and take me out to lunch. "I told him that I could go to lunch as well, and he told me he did not want me there. The cheek of him," laughed Henri.

I was so excited and looked forward to seeing Andre on our own. After picking me up, we stopped at an Italian restaurant for pasta and a drink. Andre and I got on so well together. We could talk and laugh, never once getting bored. Andre headed towards the coast and parked up near a small cove, and we gently strolled along the sea front.

It was not long before we reached the stone promenade shelter that we had used previously. "At the moment, this is the only place I can bring you to for us to have some privacy," said Andre. "The yacht has engineers on, so we don't even have her. I shall seriously have to arrange something more in keeping with us needing privacy and comfort. Any suggestions?" asked Andre as he kissed me gently.

"For the time being, this will do fine. I just want to feel you, as the saying goes, close and dirty." We both giggled as Andre said, "Come on, Christine. Hold me close and closer still."

As the weeks came and went, we took all opportunities to meet up on our own. Our paths would cross at dinner invites, dinner dances, shows, bars in town, and horse races. We mixed in the same social circle, so we were always going to be seeing each other on a regular basis. We would dance together, we would have drinks together, and we would stand in corners and chat and flirt together. We were always together. It seemed that our friends accepted us as Andre and Belle Soeur Christine, and nobody frowned upon our very close friendship. Even Henri was relaxed about our closeness. In fact, he was really pleased that we got on so well together. The downside to what was happening to us both was that the attraction we felt for each other was becoming greater and greater. If we found ourselves on our own, we would kiss, cuddle, and hold each other so close. If we found ourselves on our own with a great deal of privacy and comfort, we would have as much sexual contact as we could. There was nothing we would not try, but we never had intercourse.

The time came for Andre and his crew, including Susan, to set sail for the Atlantic trials. They were to be away at sea for at least two months, maybe three. A few days before they set off, Andre collected me from the house under the pretence of taking me to lunch so we could have some time on our own. We drove into the country and parked in a quiet, secluded are near a stream in a wooded spot. This private area gave us the opportunity to spend some very risqué sexual time together. I practically pleaded with Andre for him to make love to me, and I nearly succeeded, but right at the last minute, Andre refused, saying that it would spoil our relationship.

It was so hard for us both to say farewell. I told Andre that I was so in love with him, and Andre agreed that we both felt exactly the same. "I am so going to miss you and our times together," was the last thing that Andre said to me before he drove away from the house.

Now that there was no Andre to keep me in France, I took leave of the house and Henri, packed my things, and with doggy, I returned to my bungalow in England. I asked Henri if I could stay in England for a few weeks, hoping to revamp some rooms and enjoy the company of my children and grandchildren. He had no objection. Obviously, he would be looking forward to his womanising while I was away.

I really enjoyed my visit to my little bungalow. I felt happier than I had felt for a few years. Henri was very good to me, and although I was not in love with him, and he was always upsetting me with his antics with other women, I seemed to be coping with his adulteries quite well. I knew the main reason for this was that Andre was in my heart and in my thoughts all of the time.

As the weeks went by, I had heard nothing from Andre. I thought that he would have had made an effort to contact me by now. So I texted, "How are you doing? Are you OK? Love, Christine."

It was a few days before I received the reply. "Fine, hope you are OK." That was it! I sensed something was wrong, but I had no way of finding out what it could be.

I waited a week or so and sent this text: "How long before you are back home?"

The reply to this was, "Not sure." Now I knew something was wrong. Maybe that Susan was providing Andre with as much love, sex, and understanding as he needed, and I was just surplus to requirements now.

I was thrilled with the alterations I had had done on my bungalow, and after the decorating had been finished, I returned with doggy to the house in France. Henri was very pleased to have me back and was very loving and attentive towards me. I still had had no proper contact with Andre, and I feared the worst. "Have you heard from Andre? "I asked Henri.

"Yes, they have done really well and have been chosen to take part in the cross Atlantic trials," said Henri.

"When are they home?" I asked.

"Very soon," said Henri.

A couple of weeks later, I called on Trudie for lunch, and she said she had some news about Andre. Trudie said that because the horses had been moved to John Preston's stables while Andre was away, she had not seen him, but she had heard that he was back safe and sound and had moved into a modernised Victorian apartment near Paris with … I held my breath. In fact, I could not breathe. "Yes, Susan, his crew member!" exclaimed Trudie.

I was shocked and terribly upset. I could not understand why and how this had happened. I had to try to pretend with Trudie that I did not care, but I was breaking up inside. It hurt so badly. I was upset, and I was angry. What was I to do? Obviously, I could do nothing. I was married to his brother. His life had nothing to do with me. How could he do this to me?

When I returned to the house that evening, I told Henri what Trudie had told me. "Do you know anything about this?" I asked Henri.

"I had heard he was with that female crew member, but I know nothing else as I have not seen him yet. Good on him. It is about time he got himself a woman in his bed" replied Henri.

That night, I could not sleep. I was not upset then. I was more angry and bewildered. How could Andre, who said he loved me, treat me this way? Had I not meant anything to him at all? Well, these circumstances were far out of my understanding of our relationship as we had left it. I just had to carry on as normal and hope that the hurt would go away.

The next day at breakfast, Henri told me that he had offered the use of a company hire car to take a group of female troupe members around Paris. One of the girls was celebrating a landmark birthday, so Henri thought it would be a decent present for her. "Why don't you go with them? You seem a little bored and fed up at the moment. It will do you good to go out for the day. You know Sharon, and she will love you to go with them all," said Henri.

I replied, "I will go with them for a couple of hours, and afterwards, I may do a little shopping trip, and I will book my own car to bring me back." With that decided, I spent the morning getting all dressed up for an afternoon in the bars of Paris.

In the third bar of the afternoon, Sharon said, "Is that not Andre, Henri's brother, over there in the corner of the long bar?" My heart started to pound, and I felt quite sick. I knew that I had to turn to look to see if it was in fact Andre. I slowly turned and glanced along the bar. Sure enough, there he was standing in the corner. He knew I was there, and as I caught sight of him, our eyes met. I felt all those delicious feelings. He winked, and I nodded. I turned to Sharon and confirmed that it really was Andre. "What a good looking sexy bloke he is. Do you not think so? Go and tell him it is my birthday. He might join us and buy us a drink or two," Sharon said excitedly. I laughed and said maybe I would but not at that moment.

I was so surprised that Andre did not come over to me. What was happening? What had I done? Was he afraid that I might upset his new relationship? I needed some answers, so I took a deep breath, retrieved my clutch bag from under the table, stood up, and walked over to Andre at the bar.

I said quietly and calmly "Hi, there. I did not know you were back. Why did you not let me know?"

Andre replied, "We arrived last week. We have been busy, to say the least." Words failed me. I stood there in silence, looking at Andre, who also remained silent. I was just about to turn and leave when Andre said, "You look great. Are you OK?"

"No, I am not OK," I replied. "Have I done something to upset you? I have missed you so much, yet you seem so indifferent to me. Why?"

Andre said, "It was your idea to put a halt to us. I was doing as you asked. What did you expect me to do?"

I did not understand what he was saying. "Sorry, I really don't know what you are saying. What do you mean? Are we at cross purposes here?" I asked bewildered. Andre grabbed my hand and placed my fingers in his mouth. I felt a thrill run through my whole body. Very quietly, I said, "Talk to me, Andre. I feel like I am breaking up inside."

Andre put his arms around me, kissed me passionately, and said, "I think that Henri misled me when he told me that you wanted us to cool our close relationship. Someone had told Henri that we had been seen having sex in my car. Although Henri said he did not believe that, you, on the other hand, did not want to be talked about in such a manner, so you asked Henri to tell me to put a halt to our close relationship. I was only doing what I thought you wanted me to do. I have been so miserable, and I have missed you so much that it hurt. Forgive me, I should have spoken to you rather than just accepting Henri's version. He made out that you were in the room when he told me on Skype, just off camera, so I had no reason to think that you were not really there. I believed everything Henri said. This time, he really did get the better of me. So you knew nothing of all this? Why did you not try to contact me?"

I explained that I had texted him a few times, but he had not responded to those texts. I told Andre that Trudie had told me about his moving in with Susan, so I presumed that he no longer wanted me. "Why arrange an apartment for you and Susan when you and I could have had the apartment so that we could use it to be together now and again? I am so hurt. You have really let me down big time," I said, trying not to break down.

"I agree. I have let you down, but I promise I will never let you down again," promised Andre.

"No, you will never let me down again because I will not give you the chance again," was my answer. I turned to go back to Sharon and the party of girls, but Andre would not let go of me, demanding that I go with him to his car. I did not want to cause a scene, so I went with him and got in his car.

As we drove away, I asked where we were going. "The apartment," answered Andre.

"No bloody way. You must be joking. I am not going to have your apartment shown to me under these circumstances. Have you no regard for my feelings?" I shouted.

"I have nowhere else I can take you, so needs must … I need to be with you, on our own. I will put all this right, just give me that chance," replied Andre.

We arrived at the refurbished Victorian apartment. I told André that I really did not want to see inside them. The thought that we could have had something similar, just to give us comfort and privacy now and again, made me feel so upset. "Susan is away today, so please, let us be on our own there for a while. I need to hold and love you. I feel that if I don't make love to you today, I will have lost you forever. I feel so insecure, so please stay with me here for a few hours until I know we are both OK again," whispered Andre.

It was inevitable that we would end up naked in bed and making love. It must have been the best love-making session that either Andre or I had ever had. Every touch, every kiss, and every movement seemed to mean so much more because we loved each other. We touched, we kissed, and we climaxed together, again and again and again. While we were loving each other, I heard a door bang close. Our emotions were running so high, and afterwards, we held each other so close. "We crossed the line Andre," I said slowly.

"Yes, and I don't care," was Andre's response. I then told Andre about the noise of a closing door. "It could have only been Susan. I had better call her and make sure. I do not care what she says or does to me, but I must not let her name you. She must not name you."

Within minutes, Andre had spoken to Susan. He finished the call and turned to me. "She has already told Henri what we were doing. I thought we were all over before, well we are now," remarked Andre. His phone rang again. "Oui, Henri, oui."

"Henri wants to see us both now," Andre told me.

We both dressed in silence. I could not think straight.

Andre and I sat on the bed and cuddled. "I don't know what is going to happen now," said Andre. He continued, "I think this is the end of us seeing each other. Do not worry about Henri. He will not hurt you. Henri and I, over all our previous years, have had many break ups, but we have always made up. It will seem bad for us at the moment, but things will settle down. I love you, Christine, and I know I am really going to miss you. I will do my best to see you, but it is not going to be that easy. If you are frightened or things get really bad with Henri, phone me. I will come and make sure you are safe, but Henri would never hurt you. I can guarantee that. It is not in his nature. Are you OK?"

I replied, "No, I am not OK. I am in love with you, and the thought that it is now all over between us is breaking me up inside. The thought that I might never be able to meet you and hold you is breaking my heart. The best that could happen now is that Henri tells me to pack my bags and leave for good and return to England. He might then divorce me. I hate him and his womanising. I hate the house, and I hate how lonely I am living there. Meeting you and loving you has been the only thing that has kept me there up to now."

Andre said quickly and quietly, "We can leave now together and start a new life, but we are too old for that. Henri would ruin me and my family, and he would ruin you too. We have to face up to what we have done. Things will get better over time. I promise you that I will make sure you are all right."

As I sat on the side of the bed, Andre bent down in front of me and held my hands close to his mouth. He said, "I swear on all that is sacred to you and all that is sacred to me that one day, I will come for you. We shall be together as it should be. We shall have the retirement together that we can now dream of. It will take time for me to sort all the legal arrangements such as the divorce from Trudie and the safe-guarding of my shares in Henri and my business. It could take a year or more. What I want you to do is not to give up on us, not like I did. Any opportunity I get to contact you I will take, but if you have no contact from me for weeks or even months, please do not give up on us. I love you so much. I cannot live without you."

"I shall be with Susan for a while yet. Please listen to me! Susan and Trudie have been friends for a long time. I have been with Susan for over six years now. Susan has always been classed as my mistress. When I approach the subject of a divorce from Trudie, a good settlement and the thought that I might be moving on and marrying Susan will help my case, but if I were marrying you, there would be no chance of a divorce. I have to stay with Susan and aim to get that divorce. You then can try to get yourself in a position to divorce Henri. I know all this sounds so unlikely, but we have to try at least," said Andre.

"It will upset me so much thinking about you and Susan being intimate," I said slowly and quietly.

"Don't forget that I have to try to not think about you and Henri being intimate. As far as Susan and I are concerned, I am not really turned on by her. I have never really been turned on by women – only the few. You, I cannot get enough of. We are perfect together," he replied.

With that said, we made our way to the car and set off to meet Henri at the house. As we were driving, my hand in Andre's hand on the gear stick, Andre turned to me and said, "Hey, Christine, that sex was bloody fantastic, was it not?"

We both laughed, and I then said, "Hey, Andre, that sex was bloody fantastic, was it not?" We both laughed again.

When we arrived at the house, three security men met us. One helped me out of the car and escorted me into the house via the corridor door. The other two made sure that Andre could not get out of his car, and I could hear them telling him to leave the premises and not to return.

As I walked past the music studio, it was obvious that there was no one there. All was quiet. It seemed everyone who worked there had gone. Perhaps Henri had told them to finish early for the day. I started to feel uncomfortable about my situation.

I entered my apartment rooms to find Henri by the open windows. I closed the door behind me and sat on the nearest chair to where I was stood.

"What have you done, Christine?" asked Henri, speaking very softly. I remained silent. "What have you done, Christine?" he repeated the question, still speaking quietly and softly. "Answer me!" he said a little louder than before.

"It seems that I have been unfaithful to you, just as you have been unfaithful to me." I hissed the words out. I looked into his eyes. I felt the electricity zap me from all angles.

"How long have you and Andre been having an affair?" was the next question. He was speaking quietly and softly. "Answer me!" he demanded.

"We have not been having an affair. It just happened today," I answered.

"Then how many times have you and Andre had sex?" he continued. I looked into his eyes again, and I felt the electricity all over my body.

"I have just told you that it just happened once, and it was today," I hissed the words again.

"Why?" asked Henri.

"Why do you?" I answered back.

"Do you know how I am feeling at this very moment?" asked Henri.

"Yes, I do know how you are feeling, just as I feel when I hear you up those stairs making love to different women." I answered quietly now as I was feeling quite fretful, and the last thing I wanted to do was cry.

"Are you telling me that you have had sex with Andre to get your own back on me?" asked Henri.

"Maybe … something like that … it was you who introduced me to Andre's lovemaking. Do you remember that? The fact that you brought Andre into our marital bed? Well, who is to blame for all of this now, Henri?" I hissed the words again.

I looked into his eyes again, but this time, I saw hurt and upset. "So you know. I presume Andre told you?" said Henri quietly.

"No, he did not tell me. I actually worked it out for myself," was my answer.

"Well, I now know that you have been out to hurt me and get your revenge on me for some time now. Do you know what is going to happen now, Christine?" asked Henri.

I took a deep breath and answered. "You are going to tell me to pack my things and leave your house. I shall return home to England, and you will obviously divorce me," I said in a matter-of-fact way.

"How wrong you are. I have told you time and time again, and especially after we got married, that you will never leave me again. You must never leave this house unless you are with me. Security will be informed that you are never to be allowed to leave these premises. If you do and you do not return, I shall have your dog put down," stated Henri. "You will not be able to take the dogs for a walk unless you are with me," he added.

"I have confiscated your passport, and I have destroyed your dog's passport. As you can never return to England with your dog, it might be better for you to settle down here in the house until such time as we are mended. I shall mend us. You have really hurt me, more than you can imagine. I have treated you with love and affection, and I have given you everything you have asked for. So why?" said Henri. I looked into his eyes again. I felt the electricity pass between us. I saw hurt and upset. "You are to blame for this. Why do you always choose other women over that of your wife?" I asked. He did not answer me.

Henri said, "Come here!"

I said, "No." He walked towards me and retrieved my bag off the table. He took out my mobile phone and placed it in his top pocket. He stood behind me and placed his hands on my shoulders.

"You shall have no contact with Andre. You will not have the use of any computer," said Henri.

I replied, "I need my mobile to contact Beth, Matt, and Ruth in England. I am due to visit them next week."

"Not going to happen. Are you listening to me? Not

going to happen," whispered Henri.

He summoned Silvie from the kitchen and told her that we would be eating in that evening. He told her to make a hot dish with maybe a trifle for the sweet and to chill a couple of bottles of red wine.

Silvie looked at me in disgust and said something in French to me. It sounded pretty scolding. At this, Henri shouted at Silvie. It sounded in my broken translation that he was saying that she was only an employee and that I was the lady of the house and should be treated with utmost respect. If she did not do that, she would be dismissed. With that, Silvie scuttled away.

"You can contact your family back home in England only when I am with you," said Henri. "You have brought all this upon yourself. You smell like a dirty whore. For goodness sake, go shower and make yourself look respectable," retorted Henri. Henri left the room and slammed the door. I was relieved, and I showered, dried my hair, and dressed in some lovely pretty clothes. I thought it best to do as Henri had instructed. If I could make it up to Henri and gain his trust, I would have a better chance of returning to my home in England.

As I waited for Henri to return, I kept recalling the look on his face. I actually started to feel guilty – why did I do it? Henri was a wealthy French gentleman. He loved me and treated me with the utmost love and respect. Whatever I asked for, I received.

I knew that I loved Henri, but I knew that I was in love with Andre. The difference between them was so obvious. I loved Henri, like you love your family or your best friend, but

I loved Andre with all of my heart. I yearned for Andre. He was always in my thoughts, and I wanted to feel him, touch him, smell him, taste him, and be with him always.

It was not long before Silvie came and prepared our table for the evening meal. She would not look at me and made it clear to me by her actions that she was disgusted with me. As Henri returned, Silvie brought the hot meat dish and dished up a trif le on the side for us. She then left for the day.

We ate in silence. Henri offered me wine, but I refused. Henri poured me a large brandy and told me to drink it. I did so slowly. I did not feel like eating, but a drink I could face.

After the meal, I sat on the large sofa waiting for Henri to say or do something. "Do you want me to touch you tonight?" said Henri. I did not answer as I did not know what to say. Henri shouted "Why do you not answer me first time when I ask you something? DO … YOU … WANT … ME … TO … TOUCH … YOU … TONIGHT?" he pronounced each word slowly and with anger.

"Yes, I do," was my reply.

"Right answer. Go and get ready," said Henri.

I stripped off all my clothes, lay between the sheets naked, and waited for Henri to retire to bed. He was still working at the table, producing scores for the band members. He was also writing some new songs for the album that was due for release the following year.

I knew Henri worked very hard, but recently, I had not noticed him in any way at all. That night, as I waited for him to come to bed, I did notice him and the way he worked for the good of the band and indeed for us all.

I must have fallen asleep. I was woken by Henri kissing

me gently and seductively. I felt his hands caressing my body and then the weight of his naked body on top of mine. There was the pleasure of the thrills running through me, the pleasure of the thrill of intercourse, and the pleasure of the climax, both of us coming together as one.

We did not speak to each other; there was nothing to say. Henri had always been a fantastic lover. We were complimentary to each other in bed. He never failed to satisfy me, and indeed, I never failed to satisfy him.

I felt the weight of Henri increase, and his breathing went into sleep mode, so I moved a little so that I could breathe. We slept, wrapped in each other's arms, naked in bed. The next morning at breakfast, Henri told me that from that morning, the house was a French-only zone. He informed me that every day at ten, French tutor was to come and tutor me for one hour.

Sure enough, at ten, a woman, probably about ninety years old, came to the large lounge and immediately started her quest to have me speaking f luent French. From that day, I had a hunger to learn French. Every day, the tutor left me pieces of work to translate, words to learn, and work sheets to complete, all of which had to be done before the next day's tutorial.

As the days went by, I found French increasingly easy. I was holding conversations with my tutor. I was holding conversations with Silvie, and best of all, I was holding conversations with Henri. The French language became second nature to me. My only weakness was that I could not understand French if it was spoken quickly. I had to ask people to speak slower; otherwise, I would not be able to understand them. It worked a treat. To be able to spell written French conversations was definitely a no-go area, but as long as I was speaking French to a good standard, that would suffice.

During this time of my house arrest, probably around the third day, after my tutor had left, Andre came. All of a sudden, I looked up and there he stood, so handsome, so beautiful, and so sexy. "Hello, you," I whispered.

"How are you? I have tried many times to get in to see you, but security blocked me every time," said Andre. "You sure that you are OK? So what happened?" asked Andre. I told him of my house arrest and the threat of my doggy being put down if I left. I told him that doggy had no passport now, so he could not leave France, and Henri had told me that it would be better to stay in France if I were to keep my doggy safe.

"I shall do as Henri has asked me to do. Perhaps things will work out all right between us. Please leave before he finds out you are here. I do not want any more distress or trouble," I whispered.

Andre replied, "Henri will be here in a moment. I have asked Silvie to go fetch him. I have come to see him as well. Here is my new email address that is just for us to communicate with. You set up a new email address. Email me, and no one will be able to read our messages." With that, he pushed a piece of paper down the cushion of a chair.

Henri came bounding through the door, shouting and swearing at Andre, telling him to leave immediately or that security would throw him out. "I can throw myself out," said Andre. "I have come to see you. I need to know if you are going to enter this year's golf championship. We have won this for the last five years. If you are not going to partner me, I shall have to find another partner. God help me if it turns out to be John

Preston. I will probably kill him before the eighteenth hole," said Andre.

Andre turned to leave saying, "Think about it, and let me know. You are not answering my calls or emails. Au revoir, Christine." To my surprise, Henri said that he would partner Andre and asked what time and day was it to be. Andre told him that it was Tuesday next at nine and that he would pay for the lunch. With that said, Andre left, and Henri returned to the music studio. Perhaps things would settle down now and return to normal.

For the next few weeks, I did as Henri instructed me to do. I could speak good enough French for the tutor to be dismissed. Every day, Henri took me and the doggies out somewhere. We talked, we laughed, and we enjoyed each other's company. He told me that we had been invited to the yearly ball for gentlemen farmers. This year, it was to be held at Andre's estate. "We have to go. The band are to perform. We would be noticed if we were not to go. Questions would be asked," said Henri.

It was agreed that we would attend the ball. Henri, still not trusting me, arranged for an evening dress and accessories to be delivered to the house.

As I was still confined to the house, I pleaded with Henri to let me have the use of the gardens and woods. I told him that I just wanted to wander around for fresh air and exercise. I had an idea for a large round stone weather shelter, complete with seating, surrounded by a beautiful rose garden, again with seating. I asked Henri whether I could possibly do it as a project. When finished, I would call it Christine's Garden. To my surprise, he said it was a good idea and seemed pleased at the idea. "Choose any area you want. I shall allocate a gardener for your sole use," Henri said laughingly.

The day of the ball arrived. I was very nervous about it, but it would be great to get out and of course to see Andre. After preparing my hair, body, and nails, I tried on the evening dress Henri had gotten for me. I knew I had another evening dress of my own that I would wear if I had to do. What a shock I got! The evening dress and accessories were absolutely beautiful. It was dark bottle green of long silky material. It was off the shoulders and arms but had wide straps from the neck and top shoulders and top of the arms, holding all the dress together. It fit me perfectly. Henri helped me dress and put my diamond necklace on. I looked fantastic in the dress. Even the matching shoes fit. Knowing that I looked so good gave me the courage I needed to attend such a prestigious occasion.

As we entered Andre's estate, there were cars and limousines everywhere. The whole of the drive was lit up by all the trees being decked with thousands of tiny white lights. It looked like a wonderland. Henri squeezed my hand. "Don't be nervous. We shall have a really good night. I am proud to be showing off my beautiful wife," said Henri, smiling and winking at me.

We entered through the large front doors. The entrance hall had the stage set up for the music, and the huge hall was the dance f loor. There were people milling around everywhere in the hall and all the rooms.

Within minutes of us entering, Andre was welcoming us, only to be greeted by a very disgruntled Henri, who told him to get lost and leave us alone. They had both reared up to one another. I tried to calm the situation and so did Trudie, who came rushing out of the kitchen. "This is my house, my home, my rules," said Andre. "I don't need security to throw you out. I will do it myself. Now this has to stop! Go for a drink with Trudie, and tell your wife to dance with me. Do you hear what I am saying? Before you make a fool out of both of us, go for a drink with Trudie, and tell your wife to dance with me." With that, Henri nodded permission to me, and Andre took my hand and led me onto the dance f loor.

The band was loud and good. Andre placed both of his arms around my back, and I placed both my arms around his neck. Within minutes, Andre had pulled me close to him. I loved the delicious feelings he was giving me. He placed his face touching my face, cheek to cheek, but our lips were just touching. Every time we spoke, our lips were being touched and sending violent thrills through our bodies. I could feel his heart beating. He was pressing himself against my dress, so I could feel his body, excited and throbbing.

"Hello, you," I said. "I have been so looking forward to seeing you tonight. I was not sure whether Henri would bring you. You look stunning, you feel fantastic, and when I saw you, I thought I could do with a bit of that," said Andre.

I replied with, "When I saw you, I thought I could do with a bit of that," We both laughed and moved closer still.

"I really, really want to be on my own with you. I cannot stand not being able to hold you, love you, make love to you. I thought you might have emailed by now. Have you made a new email address?" asked Andre.

"No, I do not have access to a computer," I replied.

I could see Susan watching us, and I noticed her

breasts. They were huge! "I thought you said you sometimes find it hard to be turned on by Susan. You lying bastard! How could any hot-blooded male not be turned on by those breasts, especially if they are in your bed every night?" I said, grinding my teeth. "Is she still in your bed after what she did?" I asked, still talking through my teeth.

"Now please listen to me. I love you more than anything or anybody. After Susan caught us in her bed, she refused to go back there, making herself homeless. Trudie thought she was helping as she moved Susan into a room here at the estate," said Andre quietly.

I could not breathe for the jealousy and anger I felt. "Which room was Susan moved into?" was my next question. "Do not get upset. It was mine," was Andre's reply.

No words could describe the utter sickening feeling I had, so I whispered to Andre. "I thought that you and I had some really special love to share. We obviously don't. You see, when we were caught making love, you took me back to my husband, and I was placed on house arrest. You took your mistress to your home and moved her into your room and bed. Do you see where I am coming from? Fuck off, Andre. I do not want to play anymore. Find yourself someone else to make a fool of." I then walked off the dance f loor, holding back the tears. I found Henri and Trudie, and I quietly sipped a drink.

Henri walked off and left Trudie and me together. "How could you, Christine? How could you do what you have done?" Trudie sniped at me.

"You hypocrite, Trudie. I love you as one of my best ever friends. You were the one who advised me to turn a blind eye to any actions that would hurt my marriage. I took that advice and used it with you," I said quietly. I knew of Henri and Trudie's love affair, and I would have never mentioned it, but I had had enough that night.

Trudie looked so upset. "Who told you?" asked Trudie.

"Does it matter now. Leave me alone from now on. You are no friend of mine," I retorted.

"I think we are the best of friends because of the circumstances we find ourselves in. We must stick together, even if it is only for morale support," said Trudie.

"I would love that," I replied, and we hugged and laughed together. "I think we should go out next Tuesday, have a meal a few drinks, and shop. What do you think?" asked Trudie.

"I don't think Henri would let me do that," I answered.

"We shall see," said Trudie as she went after Henri to get his permission. To my surprise, she got it.

As the evening went on, I avoided Andre time and time again. As it got later and later, Trudie was very drunk. Most people had started to leave, and I was desperate to go back to the house. Henri, as usual, had gotten involved in a poker game, which usually lasted for hours. I told Henri I wanted to leave, and his answer to that was that he would book a car to pick me up and take me back to the house. He would follow later. He would not be too long.

The car was booked, with instructions to pick me up at the side entrance, and security at the house would be notified I was on my way home. By the time, I reached the side entrance, the limo car had arrived. As I entered the back seat, the other door opened and in came Andre. My driver had closed my door, and Andre said to him to drive away quickly. Andre gave him some extra euros, instructing him to stop somewhere quiet for a period of fifteen minutes or so. The driver checked with me that I was OK with those instructions, and I answered yes.

Within seconds, Andre had wrapped his large black stable coat around us, taken my knickers off and brought my dress up to my neck, taken his trousers down, and undid his shirt. From then on, I lay on the back seat with Andre on me. The urgency of that love making was dictated by the amount of time we had, which was really not enough. "Driver, keep your eyes on the road!" shouted Andre.

We had raw, beautiful sex. While we were having sex, and while we were kissing, Andre was talking to me all the time. While he was trying to catch his breath, he said "I know we should have left together that day. I am Andre, not Henri, who is so decisive. I am too laid back to think twice. I am sorry for letting you down. We will leave together in January to start a life like we originally said we would. I need you to get that email and the use of your phone or a computer as I will have to give you instructions." It was then we climaxed together. With very little time, only minutes away from the house, we dressed. Andre told me to vacate the car quickly, closing the door before security could see in it. I had to go in the house as quickly as possible, not looking back, and shower and put perfume on my clothes. We did not know if Henri was not far behind me for coming back to the house. As it was, Henri did not come home that night. His excuse was that he got tied up in a very long poker game.

I could not sleep that night. I kept recalling every word that Andre had said to me. Was he really going to have the courage to leave with me in January? I had my doubts. Would I want to leave Henri? After all, he had been the most attentive husband and lover. Would Andre be strong enough for the two of us?

After breakfast, I settled down in the large lounge, and Andre came to see me. "I could not settle last night. I was afraid I might have hurt you. I was so rough with you. Are you OK? Did I hurt you?" asked Andre. "Hello, you. You know me. I quite enjoy a bit of rough love making," I answered.

I could hear security coming with Henri. Henri bounded in the lounge, demanding that Andre leave the premises. "Do you know where Henri was last night, Christine? He was in Trudie's room," revealed Andre. At that remark, Henri went quiet, telling me that Andre was causing us problems and that the remark was untrue. Andre turned, told me goodbye, and left.

I knew in my heart that Henri had been with Trudie all night. I knew that if I were ever to have any future happiness, I had to be with Andre.

Tuesday came, and I was so looking forward to going out with Trudie and showing Henri that I could be trusted.

Trudie arrived in a limo car she had booked for the day and maybe the night, which made me laugh. After walking around the smaller shopping malls, we headed to the restaurant for drinks and a meal. This restaurant had booths rather than table and seats. As we settled down, Trudie looked past me and said "What are you doing here? You will get us both in trouble!" I turned, and there stood Andre, looking really smart, handsome, and sexy.

Andre sat in our booth next to me. Holding my hands under the table, he said "Trudie, I have come to ask for your help. I need you to help me get my brother back. I miss him terribly. He will not answer my calls or reply to my texts or emails. This has gone on long enough. Will you help me?"

Trudie replied, "What makes you think I can help you?"

"I know Henri was in your room all night last Saturday. As you know, I don't care what you both do. I just want my brother back," said Andre.

At this revelation, Trudie denied it all. "Go and talk to Susan. She is in the booth on the lower f loor," insisted Andre.

"No way I am leaving you two alone. Henri would never forgive me." was Trudie's answer.

"Go and talk to Susan," repeated Andre. "OK, stay there then!" said Andre as he started to kiss me and hold me close. I kissed him back, and it got quite raunchy. With that, Trudie stood up and left the booth, swearing at us both. We both laughed. We were just winding her up. "Are you OK? Are we still OK? If you don't manage to get your mobile back, I will get you one, so we can at least stay in touch. You will have to put it where Henri won't be able to find it," Andre said.

"No, I will get my mobile back, and I will email you. By the way, I have a really large bruise on my inner right thigh, but I have explained it away as being done when I fell onto the stacker truck," I laughed as I told him.

"What were you doing with a stacker truck?" Andre asked. I then told him about my project. "From plans to construction to landscaping of a very large round stone shelter with seating inside and outside. Flowers, especially roses, will be in abundance, and I will call this project Christine's Garden."

Andre laughed and said, "My, my, you have hidden talents."

Andre prepared to leave the booth as Trudie came back. "Do you know where Andre and Susan are going today Christine?" asked Trudie. I remained silent and waited for her to tell me. "They have an appointment with the jewellers to purchase an engagement ring. What do you think of that, Christine?" I remained.

Andre just glanced at me as he was leaving and said, "Nothing matters now, Christine, does it?" He turned back to kiss me and left.

I was so deeply upset. I did not know what to think or do. Andre did not have to do that for Susan. We were only a few months away from January. Why did Andre still keep hurting me? Would Andre really commit to me in January? I had my doubts. With that, Trudie and I left to find another restaurant.

By the weekend, Henri and I were packed and ready to go to Stockholm. We were to stop in one of the hotels with the band and troupe. When we arrived, everyone was so pleased to see us. That night, we settled down in the venue and watched and listened to the show. The band was fantastic. It was a credit to Henri and all his hard work. We were so brilliant, Henri and I together. We made love and cuddled all night.

It was about the third night of the tour. We had moved hotels to service a different venue. As the night went on, I noticed a woman f lirting with Henri. I did not say anything to Henri as I did not want to spoil the atmosphere around us. After we had retired to our room for the night, Henri said he would like to go out for a few hours and have a drinking session with some of his band members. Obviously, I could not object. When he returned in the early hours of the morning, I could tell that he had had sex with someone. I was hurt and upset, but I did not make a fuss.

That happened on most of the nights. At one point, I did confront Henri, but he dismissed it as being a perk to the fame and fortune they all had. "There are women everywhere when we are on tour. They are all up for it, but they mean nothing. You were once one of those women." He laughed as he said that and added, "You are my wife, and I really love you. Other women mean nothing, and they are jealous of what we have. Please do not go on. Do not spoil things – just enjoy the break."

I was glad to get back home. Silvie mentioned to me that doggy was a little out of sorts and had not eaten or drank anything for a day or so. With that, I called in the vets, who took blood tests and examined doggy in great length. They would have the results of the blood test in the next day or so.

I noticed that he was ill straight away. All he wanted to do was sit on my knee. All day I sat with him, stroking him and trying to make him eat or drink something. At night, I put him in bed with me. I was so worried. He was my lifeline. Nothing had to happen to him.

That night, Henri told me that we had been invited to Andre's and Susan's engagement party. Andre had booked the band and troupe for the evening's entertainment. It was for the following day, just as we had all arrived back home. Henri said he could do it and confirmed that we would attend.

I was so worried about doggie. I did not care what Andre was doing. How dare he hurt me again and again? I had had enough of them all. I had no intention of going to the elaborate engagement party. I had no wish to see Andre ever again. This was the final insult and the last time I would let him hurt me.

The next day doggy seemed much better. I was so relieved, but the vet came back to see me and explained that the blood tests had confirmed that doggy's liver and kidneys were not working. He was dying, and the kindest thing we could do for doggy was to have him put to sleep.

I sat there with doggy in my arms. He seemed fine, his eyes looking into mine. I had to make the dreadful decision to end my beloved dog's life. The pain I was feeling was unbearable.

The vet kneeled down at the side of us. Doggy went from looking into my eyes to putting his little head on my arm and going to sleep. It was a sleep that he would never wake from. I held him tight. I would not let go of him. I cried and cried.

Doggy had been with me since my first husband was alive. He had given me unconditional love and affection, and I repaid him by having him put to sleep. I deeply loved him. He was always there for me when things were going wrong. He was always there for me when I was emotionally down. He never judged me. He just loved me. I was inconsolable. What was I to do now without him? I could not stand the pain and hurt I was feeling. I kept crying and crying. He was the reason I got up in a morning. He was always there to greet me.

The head gardener came into the lounge. I knew he had come for doggy. Henri brought doggy's blanket and another large blanket to wrap around him. I let them take him. I felt empty and worthless. Nothing Henri said made me feel any better. My heart was aching. Nothing would be the same again.

I stayed in the large lounge all day. Henri knew I was not fit to go to the engagement party. He himself got ready to accompany his band and troupe. "Pull yourself together now. You will feel better tomorrow," remarked Henri. To that remark, I answered slowly and demandingly. "I will be leaving for England and home tomorrow. You will give me my passport, or as God is my judge, I will cause such a scandal about my treatment and house arrest that your reputation will be tarnished for ever. Do not underestimate me. I have now had enough." Henri turned and left.

As evening started to set in, I could not stand the thought of my little dog, all on his own, in the dark. Still terribly upset, I walked through the estate to Christine's Garden. I could see where the earth had been disturbed, so I knew where doggy's final resting place was. I sat on a bench and just sat there. For how long, I do not know. Night had fallen. I felt someone sit down beside me. It was Andre. He wrapped me up in his arms and under his large black stable coat. I was still trying not to cry.

"Have you not got an engagement party to attend?" I said sarcastically.

He answered, "How can there be one, if I am here with you?" He added, "I know exactly what you are going through. It was on my fourteenth birthday that my parents had to put my dog to sleep. I had had my precious dog since I was a baby. I thought I would never get over losing him. So I know what you are going through. "He started to gently kiss my face and my lips. "I told Susan last night that I was in love with you, so she cancelled the engagement."

"You are very cold, Christine. I really think we should go now, back to the house. You are going to be ill otherwise," said Andre.

"I do not want to leave here yet," I replied. As Andre kissed me, I kissed him back. "Make love to me now," I said. With that, Andre stood me up against the tall wall of the shelter, put his coat around us both, and made love to me.

Afterwards, I held tightly on to him, and he cuddled me. We were there for quite a while. I felt so lost, but Andre made me feel so safe. "Come, we really do need to get you back to the house. You need to be warmed up with maybe a hot bath and some hot drinks" he insisted. With that said, we walked slowly back to the house through the gardens of the estate.

As we neared the large steps at the rear of the house, I could see Henri. We started to go up the steps, and Andre said to Henri, "You need to take care of her. She is very, very cold. Perhaps a hot bath …"

But before he could finish what he was saying, Henri shouted, "How dare you tell me how to look after my wife. Get off my property, or so help me God, I will kill you."

Security was waiting at the top of the steps, so Andre left without any fuss, turned to me, and said, "Au revoir, Christine."

Holding tight to my arm, Henri escorted me to my rooms. "Have a hot bath. I will make you some food and a drink. Stop your crying, pull yourself together, and get into the bed. I will put the heated blanket on," demanded Henri. He brought me some soup and a hot drink, and he left. I did not see him again until breakfast the following morning.

At the breakfast table, Henri placed my passport on the table near me. He also gave me my phone and my iPad. "Do as you want now, Christine. I have had enough. This is not living, it is a nightmare I cannot wake from," said Henri in a slow whisper. He then left to go to the music studio for the morning.

After he left, I poured myself a large coffee, took some paracetamol for a really bad headache, and put my makeup on. I was breaking up inside, thinking about my doggy. I knew people did not understand how close as a companion a dog became, but to me, a dog can change your life for the better.

I thought of Henri and the look of utter failure he had as he gave me my passport and things. He had never given up on me. After all, he was my husband, and I knew I should respect that. All of a sudden, I knew what I had to do. I had to save my marriage. I had to respect Henri, and I had to love Henri as he loved me. I looked an absolute wreck. With that in mind, I washed and dried my hair, changed into decent smart clothes, and made myself up. By the time I had finished, I looked like a million dollars with swollen eyes.

I walked straight into the music studio where Henri was working. There were quite a few people there being directed on the stage by Henri. Henri turned to see what I wanted. "Well?" he said. I smiled and asked him what he would like for his tea. He looked surprised and bewildered, walked over to me, and held me tight, pushing me up against the wall. We kissed so passionately. It felt so great, and when he looked at me with those eyes … oh, those eyes … I just melted. "Can you feel what I am feeling now?" he whispered.

"Oh yes, I can" was my reply.

"Can you hold on to that feeling until tonight?" he whispered again.

"Oh yes, I can," was my reply.

"Then you are on a promise tonight," whispered Henri again. "Now go and leave me alone. I am working here," he said. As I turned to walk out of the studio, Henri winked at me. I felt good.

I spent the day walking the estate, placing f lowers on doggy's grave. I booked a return f light ticket to England for few days later. I made the visit for one week. I wanted to show Henri that I was no longer going to leave him. In fact, I wanted to show Henri how much I loved him. From then on, I was going to be Mrs Christine Chartress, lady of the house, wife to musician, multimillionaire Henri Chartress. I knew I would have to accept Henri's downfalls, but I would give it a go.

I would prove myself to Henri. It was only a few weeks from Christmas. I would take over the arrangements for the festive season. The mid Christmas party for all, plus children. The tree in the hall, the house decorations. The food menus, the Christmas gifts, and the caterers for our large party.

Silvie brought in our evening meal, steak and mashed potatoes Henri style followed by a trif le Henri style. There was red wine and brandy. "OK, we need to talk. I am enjoying your fussing, but I think you have an ulterior motive to all of this. Come on, tell me what it is. You are making me quite nervous," said Henri.

I told him of my week return to England. I told him I loved him so much that I was going to be his wife Mrs Christine Chartress from then on. "Just prove it to me, but I have to talk to you first. We have to understand each other better. We should have no secrets, and because of that, I am going to talk to you about Marcia," said Henri.

I listened quietly to what Henri was saying. He loved Marcia and her daughter in a different way than he loved me. "I let her down by leaving her in an unsuitable place because I did not want anybody to see me with her. She was attacked and raped and had a baby girl. I have done my best by her, and I have bought her a cottage to live in. Andre has given her a good job, and she is good at her job. If she needs anything, she calls me. Marcia has a boyfriend, and they seem quite serious. I will always be there for her and Julie, the daughter. I want to be able to buy them both a good Christmas present without having to hide them. I want you to know everything, so you will not keep chastising me and going into terrible moods. Trudie was the love of my life. I still love her – again, not in the way I love you. I cannot deny Trudie exists, so please accept her and don't chastise me and go into those moods. I love Andre so much. We have a problem there, which is you and him. If you ever decide to leave me for him, please talk to me. I don't think you will leave me for him as I know you really do love me. I shall start doing less with the band this year. I am tired so semiretirement might be the answer. We shall find a place for us, and we shall travel. I cannot guarantee that I won't have sex with other women if it is offered, but if I am not on tour as often, things might be different. Now you have to talk to me," said Henri, waiting for my response.

"Hurry with your brandy," I said. "I am going to have sex with you now, and it had better be good." We both laughed and spent most of the night in each other's arms, having sex and loving each other. I felt good, and I felt I had a purpose.

Just looking into his eyes (oh, those eyes) made me feel whole and wanted, just as it should be. We were Mr and Mrs Henri Chartress.

I knew that I had to phone Andre and tell him of my decision to give my marriage a chance. I was so nervous at the prospect of upsetting him but also of his upsetting me. I really loved Andre. I loved Henri, but Andre was the love of my life. Sometimes, I felt I could not breathe when I was with Andre. The feelings I had for Andre were so intense that I could not imagine life without him. I needed Andre somewhere in my life, but that could never happen if I were to give my marriage a chance. Henri was the strong decisive one, and Andre was the one with no courage, who just drifted through circumstances, a quiet man who did not like any confrontations. I chose my husband, a man with courage and a man who stuck by his convictions. At that moment in my life, I needed a man like Henri to give me a life I could enjoy with very little effort.

After breakfast, I walked down to Christine's Garden. I had a cry at the doggy's grave. After sitting there for a while, I dialled Andre's number. "Well, hello. So you have your phone back. Great! How are you?" said Andre. I tried to speak, but nothing came out. I was trying not to get emotional. "I don't like the sound of this silence. Talk to me, Christine," said Andre.

"Do I have to say it?" I said quietly with a slight sob in my voice.

"Yes, you do," was Andre's answer.

"I am going to give my marriage another chance," I said. There was no response from Andre. "Are you still there?" I asked.

Andre replied talking very quietly. "Yes … OK … must go, can't talk." I sensed a sob in Andre's voice, and he was gone. The line was dead.

I enjoyed my trip back home. I made arrangements for Beth, Martin, and the children to come to the house on Boxing Day and stay for five days. I also invited my Ruth and her husband. During those five days, we were to have a large party, take them to Disney for a day, and take them to the races and an after-races party at Andre's estate.

When I returned to the house, I occupied myself with preparing for Christmas and the New Year. I did everything I could to stop myself from thinking about Andre. Henri and Andre were back in touch, arranging for our large party, Andre's race meeting and party, and of course Andre's New Year's Eve Party.

Christmas Day at the house went brilliantly. It was just Henri's family. The grand =children were looking forward to meeting my grandchildren. The two older grandsons were about the same age group as my eldest grandson, so I knew they would all get on so well together. My other two grandchildren were much younger, four years for one and five months for the other.

Limousines were sent to Beth's and to Ruth's homes. They would have quite a few hours' drive to get to the house, but all arrived well before tea. Then the fun began.

Everyone settled in very well. The house was alive with noise. The next day was the day of the horse racing. Anyone who had a horse could join in the county's Boxing Day plus racing event.

Everyone at the house was to be at the races. The grandsons were especially looking forward to it as they were told they could have a f lutter on any of the horses – within reason, that is. Andre was riding in two of the races, so apparently he was favourite in those two races. It was decided I would look after the two babies at Trudie's and Andre's estate while waiting for everyone to return for the after-races meal.

When everyone had left, I quietly settled at the estate. I made my way from one of the lounges into the kitchen to make the baby a bottle. It was here that Andre entered the kitchen from the external door that led to the stable path. He was surprised to see me, saying he was looking for his clean riding boots. As he put his riding boots on, I felt uneasy. I did not know what to say, and I could feel my face blushing. Andre came over to me and looked at the baby I was holding. He commented how beautiful she was. The closeness of his body, the smell of his sweat, and the feel of his breath as he spoke to me sent shivers all over me. "Well, have to go. See you later," he said as he went towards the door.

"Good luck with your races," I said politely. He stopped, turned, came back over to me, held my face in his hands, and kissed me like he had me before. The passion we both felt was undeniable. He turned and returned to leaving through the external door. He stopped again, turned, and said, "We are far from being through. I know it, and you know it." With that statement, he left.

After the racing, everyone returned to the estate where Trudie had arranged a meal. It was a sit-down, four-course meal served in the largest of dining rooms. All of us had a truly wonderful night. Andre was with Susan the whole of the night. I stayed out of his way. We then returned to the house.

The next day was a trip to Disney. Cars picked us up early and brought us all back late at night. It was a superb day. The following day was the day of our mid Christmas party. Everyone was invited, including all the band and troupe members and their families. Other family members, neighbours, and friends, in fact anyone at all, could attend this party. The party had everything – plenty of food, drink, music, and fireworks. It started early to accommodate small. After their bedtime, the adult party really began. It was wonderful. My party of relatives had an absolute ball. Andre and Susan enjoyed it, and Andre stayed well away from me.

It was not long before the limos were taking my guests home. It had been a great success. Henri was so proud of me for playing hostess with such grandeur and confidence. Things felt so good between us.

At last, New Year's Eve was upon us. The celebrations, as usual, were to be held at Trudie and Andre's estate. The livestock had been taken elsewhere so as to allow for a huge firework display. Henri dressed in his evening suit, and I was dressed in my evening dress. Henri looked so handsome, and even though I say it myself, I looked fantastic. I was determined to show Henri that I truly was making an effort, and I wanted him to be proud of me, his wife.

There seemed to be thousands of people at the estate when we arrived. It was not long before Andre greeted Henri with hugs and handshakes. Andre asked Henri for permission to ask me to dance, and of course, we danced.

As the band played, Andre and I danced. We jived, we waltzed, and we behaved ourselves. Andre acting like a true gentleman, making small talk, and we laughed together at some of the more outlandish evening dresses.

When I returned to Henri, he had key number seventeen that Trudie had given him. It was the key to a room that we could use for the night instead of ordering a limo and going back to the house. I placed the key into my small purse as Henri was most insistent that he was to join a large poker game. I was to be the first to need to go to the room.

The night was brilliant. There was good music, good food, and plenty to drink. Before the fireworks display, which was Andre's favourite to do things, Andre asked me to dance. "Are you staying the night?" he asked.

"Yes," I answered.

"Have you got a room?" continued Andre.

"Yes," I replied cautiously.

"What room number?" Andre continued.

"Why?" I said cautiously.

"Just tell me what your room number is," Andre said, most insistently.

"Seventeen, and I know I am going to regret this," I said slowly.

Andre laughed and said, "I promise that you will regret nothing." He laughed again, winked, and left to set the fireworks display off.

It was midnight and the dawn of a new year. Everyone was watching the fireworks display and wishing everyone a happy new year. All night, Andre had been surrounded by beautiful women and Susan, of course, who never left his side. I felt a little jealous that I had received practically no attention from Andre, but that was how it should be. After the fireworks display, I didn't see Andre. I told Henri I was retiring to the room, and he then went to join a large poker game.

I was curled up fast asleep in my room when a knock came on the door. Presuming it was Henri, I opened the door, but there was Andre looking very pleased with himself. "You must be joking," I said scoldingly.

"No, now just listen to me," said Andre, still looking rather smug and smiling at me all the time. He continued. "I have a key to room eighteen. Now, come with me to the en suite. The en suite has interconnecting doors. These rooms are connected. They are usually used for families. You and I can play together in room eighteen for a couple of hours. If Henri comes back early, all you have to do is return to seventeen, and I will lock the interconnecting door. Now, do you want to come and play with me in room eighteen? Yes or no? Bear in mind that no is not an option!" We both laughed, and what followed was two hours of love, passion, and pleasure.

Henri returned to me at six the next morning. After a couple of hours of sleep, Henri decided that he wanted to return to the house and not stay for breakfast in the dining room at the estate. We made our apologies to Trudie and Andre, saying goodbye to the guests that were there in the dining room. Susan said nothing, but from the look she gave me, I knew she knew about Andre and me that night. I thanked Andre for a wonderful New Year's Eve, the best I had ever had, and he remarked the same back to me. We left.

CHAPTER 6

Henri Taken Ill

When we were settled back at the house, I asked Henri whether he wanted Silvie to prepare us something to eat before she finished for the day. All of a sudden, Henri said, "Christine, I do not feel very well. In fact, I feel bloody awful. I don't know whether to call our doctor or not." Looking at Henri, I could see that he was sweating profusely. I took his temperature, and I was shocked to find that it was very high.

"Take your clothes off," I said. "Put on these shorts and shirt, and I am going to wrap some cold wet towels around you to try to bring your temperature down." I made him drink some cold lemonade and take some paracetamol. "If you do not feel any better by dinner, I will call the doctor," I said. "You must have a virus, like a flu," I said, and Henri agreed.

A couple of hours later, Henri was a little better, but I was getting very concerned. He was sleeping all the time, and his temperature was not going down. I noticed his lips looked a little blue and that his fingertips looked a little blue. Straight away, I started to wake him up. He was very groggy. "Henri, start coughing for me! Keep coughing! Move your arms and hands. Do not go back to sleep! Do you hear me?" I shouted. I ran down the corridor to the front door. I was shouting for the security, who came running to my assistance. "Phone for an ambulance. Henri needs an ambulance now, and I need one of you with me now," I said as I ran back up the corridor and into my rooms.

By the time I reached my rooms, Henri had slumped over on the bed. I told security to help me sit him up and try to wake him. "Keep him awake any way you can," I said to the security man. It was obvious that Henri was drifting in and out of consciousness. I grabbed my bag and all the phones, and within minutes, the ambulance had arrived.

The medics were ready with all the machines that would detect a heart attack. Drips were put up, and an oxygen mask was on his face, and in no time at all, we were speeding towards the hospital. En route, I phoned Andre. "Andre, Henri has been taken ill. We are in an ambulance on the way to St James's Hospital," I said with a shaky voice.

"On my way," replied Andre.

I don't know why, but I also phoned Father Michael. I told him of my concern for Henri, and I asked him to go to St James and administer last rites to Henri. Even if he did not need them, it was like an insurance policy, better to have than not have.

Henri was made comfortable in admissions, and during his conscious times, he instructed me to write down the combination to the safe at the house. He instructed me to take everything out of the safe, especially my diamond jewellery. He said he did not want them to go into the estate if anything happened to him. He asked me to bring his bank app up on his phone and help him transfer most of the money he had in his account into my account. He told me he did not want any of his money going back into the estate and that I would need it if anything happened to him. I held his hand, and I looked into his eyes. There was no fire or electricity there. I could see nothing, and Henri took a turn for the worse. Alarms were going off in all directions, and Henri was rushed off to intensive care. I was taken to a relative's room and told to wait there until they had some information for me.

After looking into his eyes, I knew that Henri was not going to survive. The relative's room was cold and bleak. I stood by the window, looking out onto the gardens. I felt dead and cold inside, and I did not know what to do. I said a few prayers, but they did not make me feel any better.

Just then, Andre came rushing in. "Well, what is happening?" he said. I told him everything that had happened. He was quiet for a little while, and in an unprovoked attack, he shouted "We have done this to him! We have made him ill. We have broken his heart. I shall never forgive us if he does not recover from this. We should have known better."

"Don't be so ridiculous," I replied. "I don't think Henri will survive this. I don't know what it is, but you cannot die of a broken heart."

"Well, our mother died of a broken heart, so don't you try to be smart with me," was Andre's answer to me.

The door to the relative's room opened, and in walked a doctor and a couple of nurses. "Mrs Chartress, I am sorry to inform you that your husband died ten minutes ago," said the doctor.

I felt nothing. I could see people, but I could not hear what they were saying. I could see Andre on the f loor. The nurses were trying to lift him up. It took a while for me to come round. The doctor was telling me that Henri had a viral infection that had travelled into his heart. It resulted in a massive heart attack that Henri could not survive.

I went towards Andre. I needed him, and I presumed he needed me. "Don't come near me. Leave me alone," came Andre's response. I froze. Andre really meant what he said. He must have really believed that we had caused the death of his beloved brother, my husband.

One of the nurses said she would take me to Henri, who was having the last rite administered to him by Father Michael. I walked in the room, and Henri was wrapped in pale blue sheets. He looked asleep. I kissed him and held his hands. Father Michael continued to pray over us. I felt like a robot.

Andre entered the room. He was distraught. He asked Father Michael for absolution as he was feeling guilty. He said that we had committed adultery and that he needed some kind of forgiveness as Henri could not forgive us now. Father Michael heard Andre's confession and continued to forgive him his sins. He turned to me and asked me if I wanted to confess my sins. I said I did not. "I am not sorry for anything I have done, so it is pointless to ask for any forgiveness."

I was so disgusted at Andre's behaviour. I asked Andre if he would come with me back to the house, so I could collect a few things. I told him I did not want to go back there on my own. I had nobody else to ask. "Father Michael will take you back," Andre said. "I need to be on my own now — not with you," Andre said most hurtfully. I turned and walked away with Father Michael. I swore I would never forgive Andre for treating me that way. I needed Andre more than I had ever needed anyone ever, but he let me down.

Father Michael drove me back to the house. On the

way, he was good enough to give me a pep talk. He told me that all through history, a married woman falling in love with her husband's brother had been noted as the cause of wars, murders, changes of rulers, and more. He smiled and said, "That's life."

I instructed Father Michael to arrange Henri's funeral with Andre. I would not be around as I intended to return to England and my home. I needed people around me who loved me and could support me in my hour of need. I had nobody at all to rely on in France. I obviously could not turn to Henri's family.

I asked him to pass on this message to Andre. "You were the only person in the whole wide world who could have comforted me in my deepest hour of need. You gave me the greatest betrayal ever. I will never be able to forgive you. I have nobody at all in France, so I am returning to England and my home, where I have people who love me and will support me. Arrange for Henri's funeral with Father Michael. I do not want to know anything. Henri has gone now, so what the hell! You sort things out. As far as I am concerned, you are his next of kin. Au revoir, Andre. I hope we never meet again."

While en route to the house, I phoned Henri's daughter to give her the bad news. I asked her to tell her brother. I then phoned to arrange a limo to take me via Le Shuttle back to England. I instructed them to make sure the driver had his passport with him. The car would be with me within the hour.

I entered the house through the side door. There were people waiting there for news. I told Silvie that Henri had died. I instructed the head of security to lock down the house. Nobody was to be allowed in unaccompanied. All Henri's music and manuscripts had to be protected until Andre had sorted something out.

I walked alone across the large hall towards my rooms. It was so quiet. Would I ever see Henri's ghost? No, but I did feel his spirit. I threw everything I had into two large suitcases. I took just four photographs, and as Henri had instructed me, I opened the safe and took all of its contents, including all my diamond jewellery. The car had arrived, and I left, hopefully forever.

I curled up on the back seat of the limo. I cried and cried. What was I to do? By the time I arrived home, I had made some decisions. I never wanted to return to the house. I needed to contact Henri's lawyers, so as to establish what was what. Once I knew what provisions Henri had left me, I could then proceed with the next step.

Once home, the whole family went into mourning with me. My daughter would not stop crying. I felt that I could cry no more. My mobile started ringing. Every phone call from Andre I ignored. I never wanted to have anything to do with him again. I chose whom to speak to and whom to ignore. At one point, I turned my phone off all together. I kept watching Henri's phone. Nobody of any importance had rung him. I needed Henri's phone as it had all the important numbers, including Henri's lawyer.

After a few days, I began to feel more like myself. I gave myself confidence to carry on with style. I knew Henri was gone forever, and I missed him, but it was Andre I missed the most. I missed Andre all the time. I was always trying to stop myself from thinking about him. At night, I would wake in a a cold sweat, thinking that Andre was there with me, holding me, kissing me, and making love to me. I was so disgusted with myself. I knew I had to avoid all future contact with him.

At last, the call I had been waiting for came. Father Michael rang to tell me that Henri's funeral was to be held on the Wednesday the following week. "You must be there, Christine. You must also be there, the day before, as Henri will be lying in state in the large hall. There is so much interest, especially from the paparazzi. There will be two condolence books as we expect a great volume of people to come to pay their respects. You have no choice. You must return and do your duty as his widow," insisted Father Michael. I shuddered at the thought of going back into the house.

"Did you give Andre my message?" I asked.

"Yes, but he was so preoccupied that I am not sure that he took much notice of me," answered Father Michael. "I hope to see you when you return," he said before hanging up.

I knew that I would have to attend Henri's funeral and Henri's lying in state, so the next time Andre called, I answered. I was so nervous, I was so angry, and I was so lost. "What the bloody hell are you playing at?" Andre said. "Get yourself back here, and act as you should – if you haven't forgot, Henri's widow," said Andre, talking through his teeth and sounding very angry indeed.

"Don't you dare talk to me in that tone," I demanded. "For me to return, I need you or someone to book me into a hotel nearby the house for the night of the lying in state. I require only one night as I shall be returning home after the funeral the day after. Send me details of the hotel. I will find my own way there," I said and hung up. Andre tried phoning three more times, and each time, I ignored the call.

A hotel, address, and telephone number were texted to me. I booked f lights from England to France return for the dates I had been given. My daughter and I spent days trying to buy appropriate outfits. At last, I was sorted and packed. On the day, I boarded the plane and landed in France at about ten in the morning. As I walked into the arrivals lounge, there he was, looking fantastic, aff luent and sexy. Andre Chartress, in all his glory.

It was pointless ignoring him. I had not told him when I was to arrive as I was going to make my own way to the hotel. Could it be that he was to greet someone else at the arrivals? I knew I had to stand tall and assertive, so I walked over to him and said "Am I to presume you are here to meet me and take me to the hotel?"

"Yep," was his answer. Nothing more.

We walked out of the airport. Andre was helping me with my luggage. I watched his body move. I looked at his beautiful hands. I could feel my body going into Andre meltdown. I ached for him. I did not want a conversation with him after what he had done, so we travelled in silence for a while.

"I have a telephone number of the nurse who was the last person to speak to Henri on that terrible night. She told me that Henri had an important message for me. It is written on that piece of paper you are holding. If you want, phone that nurse and talk to her. She made me feel a little better that night."

The message read, "Please, please, Andre, take care of my Christine, and love her."

"Trudie has prepared a room for you. She wants you to

stay with us. What do you say?" asked Andre

"No, take me to the hotel as I instructed."

"If it is something to do with Susan being there, she is quite prepared to stay elsewhere," added Andre.

I was so angry with Andre. "I do not give a damn about Susan or the arrangements Trudie has with her. It is you I do not want to be near. I do not want to even talk to you. You committed the ultimate betrayal. You turned me away when I needed you most. You knew of my fear at being left alone. Well, how alone can you be when your husband has just died? Fuck off, Andre, and leave me alone," I said slowly and with purpose.

"So that is a no to the room at the estate, is it?" said Andre rather smugly.

We arrived at the hotel. It was a beautiful country hotel in its own grounds. As Andre helped me out of the car, I tingled from head to foot. I could see the same reaction in Andre. I have got to ignore him.

Andre helped me with my case, turned to get back into his car, and said, "I will pick you up at three-thirty. We have from four until five for the family to have private viewings. Be ready!"

We arrived at the house by four. I knew that this was going to be upsetting, and I had tried to prepare myself for the viewing. What I did not expect was to see hundreds of people, press and television, camped outside the front gates. There was a line of people queuing to enter the house and include their condolences in the books provided.

We entered by the side entrance. Andre took me to the large lounge via the outside patio area. As I entered the lounge,

I could see all the faces of people so upset and inconsolable. I stood there, wanting to cry myself, but I held firm. Trudie came over and hugged me, crying all the time. I could do without all this. I made my way straight to the hall door and went in. I heard someone say it wasn't time yet, but it was my time regardless.

What met me was the most beautiful display of candles, thousands of them. Henri was there, all dressed up and looking so peaceful. People were still milling around, but I did not care. I put my head on his chest, and I could no longer control myself. I cried and cried. I tried talking to Henri, but all I kept doing was crying. I felt Andre getting hold of me, putting his arms around me and taking me away from Henri. "Just give yourself a minute," Andre whispered.

"Who the hell do you think you are to tell me what to do?" I said venomously.

I walked around the hall. The candles were so beautiful. The whole of the hall had been transformed into a fairyland of candles. I went to find Trudie to thank her for the most spectacular display. I presumed that Trudie was responsible for it, and I was correct.

I made a simple entry in one of the condolence books. It read, "That is it. Goodbye. I will always love you, and I will never forget you. Your Christine."

I called to Andre, asking him to take me back to the hotel, there and then. I did not want to wait there a moment more than I had to do. Andre helped me into his car, deliberately holding me tighter than he needed to do. "I have told you before. Fuck off, Andre. Leave me alone," I said with determination, even though I was desperate to hold and love him.

At the hotel, after Andre had helped me out of his car, again deliberately holding me tight, I looked into his eyes. As he winked, I found myself smiling at his cheek. "That is better," said Andre. "I really want to hold you. Any chance I could take you to your room?" he whispered. I just shook my head and walked away. "I will collect you at nine-thirty tomorrow. It is going to be a really bad, bad day," said Andre who then started to cry. He composed himself as he drove away.

CHAPTER 7

Funeral and Life After the Death

The day of the funeral arrived. I prepared myself and dressed in a lovely black suit, white blouse, and black hat with netting around. At least the netting hid my eyes. I wore all my diamond jewellery. I was dressing for Henri and nobody else. I had a large white f lower, which I placed on one of my lapels. With all my makeup on, I finished with Henri's favourite perfume. I was ready, but I was breaking up inside. I knew I had to stay firm and strong. I also knew that it would be Andre who would go to pieces. I felt for him. He had lost the only person he had ever loved.

As we followed the coffin car, I glanced at Andre. He seemed so lost. When we followed the coffin into the church, I held my hand out to Andre. Without hesitation, he took it and did not let go of it until the whole of the mass and graveside burial had finished. Even then, he still held on tight to me. "You cannot go home today, Christine. Tomorrow, I have arranged meetings with our lawyers for a private will reading and meetings with the company's accountants. We have to make a start of finalising the business arrangements. I do not know what you will want to do, but tomorrow is soon enough for decisions."

When all the service was over, I stood by the graveside, Andre still attached to my hand. "You need to come back to the house for the wake," said Andre. "People are expecting it of you. The band and troupe are to do a farewell tribute to Henri." At this, Andre broke down. I held him close, but there was no comforting him. With my face so close to his, he kissed me, still crying. He kissed me again and again and again. We held on to each other for ages.

I did return to the house as a sign of respect for all the talented people who were there for Henri. I waited in the lounge area while Andre went onto the stage and spoke to all the guests. It was then I heard a chanting of my name. In response to that, I made my way along a path people had made for me. I stood on the stage, looking down at the silent crowd.

I said, "I look at all your faces. The sadness I feel I can see in you all. Nothing will ever be the same again. None of us know what the future holds for us. Henri always controlled our futures. Well, now we have to take control ourselves. Andre will always be here for you. I am to say goodbye and return to England. I will never forget you all, such talented, beautiful people. Love one another, and enjoy today because tomorrow may never come." With that said, I cried as I left the stage. I asked Andre to take me back to the hotel. I had had enough for one day.

When we arrived at the hotel, Andre asked if he could just stop with me for a little while. "Can we just sit in the gardens with a coffee and a brandy or two?" he said. "I have nowhere to go and no place to be," he added.

"Why not?" I said, and we sat amongst the f lowers getting drunk. As night came, the hotel arranged for Andre to be taken back to the estate by limo. He was very drunk, and so was I. He arranged to collect me the next day at nine. His car was already at the hotel, so all he needed was a lift to the hotel if he could work that one out. He was very, very drunk.

The next morning, I woke up with a massive headache. I made myself eat some breakfast, and I drank loads of orange juice. I could not remember much of the previous night. I did know that Andre did not stay in my bed and that he took a limo back to the estate.

Andre arrived to take me to his offices to meet our lawyers and the company's accountant. He looked terrible. "I have a terrible hangover," he said. "I blame you for letting me drink so much. I don't remember much, but I do remember your saying that you forgave me and that we were now OK. You also said that you needed me, wanted me, and loved me."

I looked at his face. "You must think I am stupid to believe all that rubbish," I said as I laughed at his attempt to sort us out.

When we arrived at the office, everyone had arrived. Sat the in board room, I listened to the will reading. It was all as Andre had said it would be apart from a house that Henri had left me. The will read, "To my beautiful wife, Christine. A wedding present from me, a Georgian property called Laburnum Cottage to be renamed Chartress Cottage. It's a wreck of an old house, but as a project, you will bring it back to life. Do with it what you want to do. Sell it if you want, but give it a chance first."

I knew which property Henri was referring to. It was an old Georgian we had found. I had fallen in love with it, but Henri said it was not the right time for it. To think that Henri had bought it for me anyway. Why had he never mentioned it to me? I was thrilled about this. It was just what I needed to give myself a purpose. With half of the Chartress Company and my own property, I was more than pleased, and I felt secure. I did not know what the value of the Chartress Company was, but I knew it ran into millions. I requested, from the company accountant, a statement of affairs and the latest profit and loss account and a balance sheet. I showed them that I knew what I was talking about and that they should not take me for granted. Andre sat there, looking quite smug. He looked very proud.

With the meeting and will reading well and truly over, all forms signed and instructions given, Andre called the meeting to a close. Everyone left, leaving Andre and myself alone. "Don't take me on, Christine," demanded Andre.

"I think I already have, Andre." We both looked at one another and then we both laughed.

"Come … let us go look at this property," said Andre.

"Yes, I am so excited. I have seen it before with Henri," I said. "I know, and I have seen it before, when Henri asked me to purchase it for you. I was sworn to secrecy," revealed Andre.

As Andre helped me get into his car, the delicious, thrilling feelings ran through my body. Andre and I had always had a great sexual attraction between us. Making love with Andre was effortless. He never ceased to thrill me, please me, and satisfy me. All it had ever done was bring us heartache and trouble. I was determined that from then on that I was not going to let my feelings take over my life, and I was not going to forgive Andre that easily.

We arrived at the old, broken down, empty Georgian house that was now to be called Chartress Cottage. We opened the large old gates and drove up to the house. All the gardens were overgrown.

With keys in hand, I opened the front door. In silence, Andre and I walked through the house and out to the back. The swimming pool was damaged and overgrown. We walked around the large stables. Most of them had fallen down. Back into the house, none of the bedrooms had en suites. There was only one family bathroom. There was no central heating, and no kitchen as such. In fact, it needed to be gutted, just keeping some of the original features.

This house had set my heart on fire. It was a project I could throw myself in to. As we entered the large master bedroom, Andre made a dive for me, throwing me onto the old bed and mattress that had been left. There was no foreplay – just sex. The feeling of his hands under my top clothes. The feeling of his lips pressing hard on mine. The urgency of the intimacy that followed was so exciting. We both climaxed with such a powerful finish.

As we lay there, Andre whispered, "Do you know what we have just done, Christine?" I stayed silent. "We have just christened our new home," he said. Andre said he could see us living in that house. "I would like two babies, two blond babies, the sort of babies that have large f loppy paws, usually called golden receiver pups. They would sleep on the hearth rug in front of our fire in winter. In summer, they would have their own pen. I would train them, and you can spoil them." We both laughed with excitement.

Andre continued. "Our grandchildren and our great-grandchildren would love it here. We shall have an open house all the time. We shall have noise and laughter, and this will bring this beautiful mansion back to life. I would have a good working stable with a stable man. We shall have a gardener and a house woman. A pool man will call at intervals. We shall be together at last, I shall be retiring so we will live as one, and we will not let life get in the way."

As we lay there on the old broken bed and mattress, I had to forgive him, but I knew that he would let me down again. He had let me down so many times that I was frightened for our future. He could so easily change his mind about all of this. I knew that he loved me, but he did not seem to have any self-courage. I just had to put all my hope and dreams into Andre Chartress.

It was to be his last year on the racing yacht. It was getting too much for him now. He wanted to sell the estate, again because it was getting far too much for him to handle. A divorce would be ideal, but that all depended on Trudie's demands. The company must be able to service her demands without causing a cash-f low crisis. Both of us would have to secure the necessary funds through our loan accounts. Susan would have probably left by then as things were not that good between them now.

We held each other for ages. We both agreed that this house was beautiful. It was agreed, that while Andre was away racing the yacht, I would take on the whole project and bring this house back to life. It would be for us to make a home in it and start to live in it together for the rest of our lives.

I was so excited and so much in love with Andre that I put my whole trust in him. He was to transfer money into my account to help me with the overall cost of the modernisation.

Then came the shock. "Christine, I need to talk to you. Please listen, and do not start to be awkward with me," said Andre. "It is only two weeks since Henri died. We have to respect him and his memory by having a respectful time of mourning. I know that Henri has been nominated for many music awards, now posthumously. The articles in most of the large tabloids and magazines are so respectful of Henri and his wife, Christine. Henri is part of France and France's way of life. We cannot afford to tarnish his image. We must not let Henri down by behaving in a way that will cause all of us pain and grief. If the media turns against you, you and our family will be torn to pieces. For all of these reasons, for the next twelve months, most of which I shall be away, we must not continue to see each other as we have been doing. I shall email you, and I shall love you every day we are apart. Please understand. Bring this old house back to life, ready for you and me. I love you so much that it hurts. We have no choice now."

I agreed in principle to everything Andre had said. We returned to the hotel, where I packed and prepared for my f light home the following day.

When I returned to Chartress Cottage, I found myself a beautiful French hotel on the nearby coast. I used this hotel every time I went to the cottage. I met some lovely people and made plenty new friends. Over the next few months, I threw myself into Chartress Cottage. I had all sorts of tradesmen working very hard for me. The list of work being done was endless.

I kept in touch with Andre constantly. Every night I would email him, telling him stories and sending him pictures of the cottage. I missed him so much, but I kept myself busy.

When he was home, we did manage to see one another. Sometimes, we were lucky to have some private time, and we did make the most of those times, but they were few and far between. Regardless, we still held onto each other, hoping that our love would survive our circumstances.

When all of the structural work had been completed and the rooms were ready for decorating, with really hot summer weather around us, I turned my interest to the outside area. The swimming pool had to be completely renewed, and the gardens had to be replanted. When all was complete, I invited all the family for a test drive.

It was fantastic to have everyone there. The children were boisterous, jumping in and out of the pool. My daughter and her husband relaxed on the new patio area. My sister and her husband loved to travel to the nearby beaches. It was all as it should be. There was still quite a bit of work to be done, but in fairness, those things were mainly cosmetic.

As I lay on a sunbed dozing, someone stepped into my sun path. I opened my eyes, and at first, I jumped since I thought it was Henri. However, it was Andre. Still handsome, still sexy, and still mine, I hoped.

"Hello, you," I said. "What are you doing here? Why did you not phone me to let me know you were coming?" I asked.

"I wanted to surprise you," he answered, looking very smug. "I did not know you had all the family here, but the children will be able to help me," he added.

"I have presents for your grandma," he said to the little ones. "Can you go into my car and bring them here? Take really good care," he added. With that, the children ran to Andre's car, which was parked around front. I could hear them squealing with delight and round the corner came bounding two golden retriever pups, all paws and tails.

I stood there, watching the mayhem the pups were causing. I did not know how to react. I had a feeling that something big was going to happen, but I dared not ask. Andre walked over to me, put his arms around me, and asked "Which room is our bedroom?" as he looked at the back of the house.

"That one there," I answered, feeling very sick and nervous. "Lovely," remarked Andre.

"I have two pieces of paper for you to read," said Andre. "Which one do you want first?" I pointed to one and Andre gave it to me. I glanced at the contents. It was a marriage license with the names of Christine Chartress and Andre Chartress. He gave me the other piece of paper. It was a divorce decree from Trudie Chartress.

Andre shouted to the older children. "Horse box vans will be here shortly. I could do with some help to settle and bed down four very lively horses." Turning to me and holding me tight, he said, "I told you, more than once, I would come for you. Well, here I am. I am home." He then added, "Come on, Christine. Hold me close and closer still."

www.ingramcontent.com/pod-product-compliance
Lightning Source LLC
Chambersburg PA
CBHW051117050726
47592CB00002B/860